THE SECRET COURIER

PART II

An Untold Gripping WW2 Historical Fiction of the Heroic British Spy Who Helped Win World War II

(Based on a True Story)

CURT O'RILEY

This book is a work of fiction. Names, characters, businesses, organizations, places, events and incidents either are the product of the author's imagination or are used fictitiously. Any resemblance to actual persons, living or dead, events, or locales is entirely coincidental.

ALSO BY THE AUTHOR

WORLD WAR II HOLOCAUST FICTION SERIES

WORLD WAR II HOLOCAUST FICTION SERIES

THE SECRET COURIER PART I

Welcome to Part II of the story. I hope you find it captivating and engaging. However, I'd like to gently remind you that this book is a continuation of the narrative that began in Part I.

To fully appreciate the depth of the characters, the intricacies of the plot, and the evolving themes, reading Part I first is encouraged.

Part I is available in the store.

Happy Reading!

CONTENTS

" Will mercy shown bring downfall near,

Or will it spark a bond sincere?"

1

CHAPTER ONE

Olivia walked down the sidewalk, her heels clicking furiously as she hurried toward the War Office. She looked down at her watch, which read 11:15. Nobody would be in the office at this time of night... Hans never stayed past 10 p.m., even on his most recent night.

She quickened her pace as she looked behind her. The street was deserted, with street lamps shining incandescently on the empty cobblestones. Still, she didn't want to stay too long and risk being noticed if someone came along.

She turned down the side road that led to the War Office's back entrance, holding Hans's keyring in her pocket. Because that was how she and Hans had left on nights when he stayed late, she decided it would be a better plan than attempting to enter through the front door. She took out the ring and fiddled through the keys until she found the one she was looking for. She twisted it into the door lock and heard a light 'click' as it opened. She slipped inside, locking the door behind her and looking over her shoulder one last time.

She glided down the long hallway that led from the back entrance to the main workroom floor, taking care not to step on her toes so her shoes' heels didn't click as loudly. She was certain she was alone in the building, but she didn't want to take any chances by making excessive noise.

When she finally arrived at the main office, she paused with bated breath, listening intently for any indication that she wasn't alone. When she heard nothing, she crossed the workroom floor to General Sinclair's office. She jiggled the door knob, which was locked. With a sigh, she realized that it would not be easy.

She slipped the hairpin that had been holding back the curls on her face into the keyhole. She'd never picked a lock before, so it couldn't be that difficult. She jiggled the knob by twisting the lock's pin. After what seemed like an eternity of wiggling the pin from left to right and up to down, she heard a click.

With a sigh of relief, she turned the knob and slipped inside the office, lightly closing the door behind her.

She stepped around General Sinclair's desk, the red oak lit by the dim glow of the moonlight shining through the office window. Her gaze was drawn to her target as she sifted through the various papers and files on the desktop.

She picked up the familiar red folder Lieutenant Hayes had given General Sinclair earlier that day and opened it, thoroughly scanning the pages. Prisoners were to be transferred from the Amersfoort camp to Vught. She furrowed her brow in bewilderment... She couldn't recall ever hearing about a labor camp in Vught. Is it new? She kept reading...Apparently, a large group of Dutch Resistance prisoners being held in the city jail will also be transferred there.

After reading the report in its entirety, she closed the folder and returned it to its original location before turning for the door, a deflated feeling overtaking her. She hoped the report would include more than just a few details about a prisoner transfer. Regardless, she would inform Harold and Cecilia... Perhaps it was more significant than it appeared.

She opened the office door, turned the lock, then slipped out and closed it behind her. She turned on her heel and walked down the hallway, twisting the knob one last time to ensure it was locked behind her.

"Who do we have here?" Olivia nearly jumped out of her skin when she heard a voice behind her. She spun around and saw four strangers standing in front of her. They certainly did not work in the office, with each man looking as surprised to see her as she was to see them.

"You're not supposed to be here," she said, squaring her shoulders and her mind racing in a million different directions. So, who were they? What exactly did they want.

"Says who?" The man who spoke before asked. He was taller than the rest, with dirty blonde hair cropped close to his scalp.

"Who are you?" She inquired, standing firm.

"I'm sure you've heard of us," he said, taking a deliberate step towards her. She examined the stranger up and down, her gaze falling on the faded orange armband embroidered with the letters 'OZO,' which was fastened around the man's sleeve.

"You're Resistance," she breathed, instantly recognising the symbol as that of the Dutch Resistance.

"Oranje zal overwinnen," the man boasted, pushing his arm out proudly to show off the band.

"Orange will triumph," Olivia declared in English.

"You know Dutch?" The man said this while taking another step towards her. "So, you're not German, you're just a traitor."

"Leave her alone," another member of the group stepped forward, his hair longer and darker than the first, and grabbed him by the shoulder. "She's not what we came here for."

"Yes, but she's seen us," the first man replied to the other. "Which means she can turn us in," he said, nodding at Olivia.

The other man looked at her, his gaze moving down her frame as if to assess her.

She reached reflexively for her bag, her gun securely clasped inside, but stopped. If she fought back or alerted anyone, how would she explain her presence at the War Office at this late hour? After all, she was not supposed to be there. If these men perceived her as a threat, pulling a gun on them was the last thing she needed to do to avoid further escalation. She let go of her bag and took a step forward.

"I won't turn you in," she stated cautiously, raising her hands.

"Hmmmm," the first man exclaimed. "I'm sure."

"I won't," Olivia shook her head and took another step towards them, her hands still raised to her chest.

"Why wouldn't you?" The second man inquired skeptically, but his tone was less hostile.

"Because," she paused, thinking about her next words. Was she really about to reveal her identity to these four strangers? She inhaled sharply and spoke, reconciled with the fact that it was her best option right now. "Because we're on the same side."

"Same side?" The dark-haired man inquired, his brow furrowed in confusion.

"Yes," she replied, nodding. "I'm working for the SIS."

"You're with the British?" The first guy inquired in disbelief. She nodded again.

"How are we to believe you?" The dark-haired guy inquired, yet his query was not frightening. She took her handbag and gently unclasped it to reveal the silver revolver within. The other three guys jumped back instinctively, waving their weapons at her.

"It's British issued," she said, giving it over to the dark-haired guy. "The fact that I didn't pull it on you the moment I saw you should be reassurance enough," she went on to say. He took it up and examined it intently in the fluorescent brightness of the moonlight shining through the window.

"Where did you get this?" He inquired, his gaze shifting from the rifle to Olivia.

"The agents I'm working for," she said simply. "For protection ... If I were to need it."

The dark-haired man's stare lingered on her for a time, then sharpened as he searched her eyes for the truth. He held out the revolver and offered it to her.

"What are you doing?" The first guy questioned, his mouth wide open, as Olivia returned the revolver and stashed it in her backpack.

"I believe her," the dark-haired guy said, turning to his friends. "Why make up such an elaborate lie when she could've just alerted the authorities of our presence?" He focused his attention back on Olivia. "You're not supposed to be here either, are you?" He asked.

"No," she said, shaking her head.

"Well, maybe we can help each other then," the dark-haired guy remarked, a slight grin appearing on the corners of his lips. "I'm Lawrence," he replied, offering his hand to her.

"Olivia," she said, grasping his hand and shaking it firmly.

"This is Calvin," he continued, nodding toward the first guy. "And this is Wolfgang and Alex," he remarked, pointing at the two boys behind him, none of whom is older than Olivia's sister.

"We're looking for something, Olivia," Lawrence whispered, leaning in as if he didn't want anybody to overhear them, even though they were still alone.

"On Christmas Day, a handful of our lads were detained for interrogation by the Gestapo. While they were being questioned, their families were detained... They were snatched from their homes without notice and transported off to God knows where. Calvin's sister and two nephews were abducted," he said, giving Calvin a sympathetic look before continuing. "We need to know where they're being held."

"I..." Olivia trailed off, her thoughts turning to the dossier Lieutenant Hayes had handed General Sinclair. The report listed several suspected Dutch Resistance members who would be transferred with the work camp inmates. Perhaps these inmates were the lost relatives of the Resistance fighters.

"Come with me," she murmured, spinning on one heel. When she returned to General Sinclair's office, she pulled out the same hairpin she had previously used to open the door and inserted it into the lock. Twisting it, the door snapped open much more smoothly this time.

"That doesn't seem like the first time you've done that," Lawrence said something in a whisper.

"It's not," she said quietly, opening the door with a creak. "Come on," she urged, entering the office with the four guys following closely behind her. "There will be a transfer of prisoners from the labor camp in Amersfoort to a new camp in Vught," Olivia said, taking Lieutenant Hayes's report from the General's desk. "Resistance members being held in the jails here in Den Haag will be transferred there as well," she said, offering the folder to Lawrence. He received it and thumbed over the pages.

"Does it mention Emily?" Calvin spoke forward, glancing over Lawrence' shoulder and reading for himself.

"No names are mentioned," Olivia answered, a sorrow running through her chest as she saw Calvin's desperation. She was all too familiar with the sense of being powerless. "But if your sister and her boys were taken because of their connection with Resistance, then I think there's a really good chance they're being taken to Vught."

"Thank you," Lawrence replied honestly, shutting the folder and returning it to Olivia when he had read it in full.

"Of course," she said with a nod.

"Your secret is safe with us," he whispered, gently squeezing her arm. "Be careful."

"You too," she said. Lawrence nodded, offering her a kind grin. With that, the four guys turned and departed the office, silently returning the way they had come.

2

CHAPTER TWO

Olivia mounted the stairs to the Winslows' front door, softly wrapping against the wood. She had left work as soon as that afternoon's conference ended and walked the short distance to the Winslows' house. The door opened, showing Cecilia's small figure.

"Olivia?" Cecilia inquired; the astonishment of Olivia's unexpected presence evident on her face.

"Can I come in?" She questioned, stepping inside as Cecilia stepped aside.

"Is everything okay?" Cecilia inquired, furrowing her brow in worry as she closed the door behind them.

"I have some new information," Olivia said, jumping right to the point. After her encounter with Lawrence and the other Resistance members, she wanted to provide Harold and Cecilia the information she had obtained during her late-night visit to the War Office as soon as possible. The move was scheduled for the next week, so there was still time to prepare a rescue operation. Perhaps the lost families of Dutch Resistance members, as well as work camp captives, can be brought to safety.

"There will be a prisoner transfer from Amersfoort to a new camp in Vught," she started as she sat in the living room, Harold and Cecilia seated opposite from her in their normal positions.

"What?!" Cecilia asked.

"We can rescue them-," Olivia said, ignoring the Winslows' perplexed looks.

"Olivia, slow down," Cecilia said again.

"We know the precise time and place... Just like the supply transports," she said, without pausing. "You can contact your people," she replied, focusing her attention on Harold. "We can help them."

"Olivia, we can't," Cecilia said, shaking her head and giving

Harold a knowing look.

"What do you mean we can't?" She wrinkled her brow, noticing for the first time since she sat down that Harold and Cecilia did not seem to share her delight for this new revelation.

"I met some Dutch resistance," she said, hoping to make them understand. "Their family members were abducted on Christmas. They will be brought to Vught next week. We can return them to their loved ones!"

"Wait, what?" Cecilia inquired in amazement. "When were you speaking to Dutch Resistance?"

"It's a long story," Olivia shook her head, not wanting to go into too much detail about her break-in attempt.

"It does not matter. Harold interjected, "We can't intervene."

"Why not?" She inquired, furrowing her brow.

"If it were our men or allied troops, we could possibly organize a rescue mission, but-" Harold started, but she stopped him short.

"But what?" She inquired, rage surging inside her. "Because they're Jews and Resistance their lives somehow matter less?"

"That's not what he's saying, Olivia," Cecilia said.

"Not in so many words," she responded, her tone harsher than she had anticipated.

"You don't understand," Harold said dismissively.

"Oh, I understand perfectly," Olivia said, her pulse thumping in her chest as she struggled to remain calm.

"No..." He shook his head in annoyance. "You don't. If we acted on every piece of information we got, where would we end? Where do you draw the line?"

"Not at the innocent lives of women and children!" She responded angrily, getting to her feet suddenly.

"You can't save everyone, Olivia," he said exasperatedly.

"No," she said, shaking her head. "But these individuals can be, and you don't mind! You are choosing to do nothing... You are no better than the men who put them in that camp to begin with." She spit out, her tone filled with contempt.

"Olivia!" Cecilia started, but Harold cut her off.

"You think I don't care, but I just see the big picture," Harold said, sitting forward in his seat with a deathly calm tone. "Something you clearly can't accomplish... Olivia, open your bloody eyes and see what we're doing here!" He pounded his fist on the side table, his voice bellowing loudly.

"Suppose we were to plan a rescue effort for those detainees and it went wrong. What happens to them, and millions of others like them, when those waging the war from inside are apprehended and killed?"

"What happens next, Olivia?" He asked, straining his teeth in desperation.

She grabbed her bag off the chair and headed toward the door. She'd had enough with this lousy job. She wanted to make a difference... to assist others. But how could she achieve one of those things if the people she worked for could turn a blind eye so casually?

"Is that all you had for us?" Harold yelled behind her.

"That was all. Am I free to go?" She questioned, turning to face him.

"Remember what you're here to do," Harold whispered, his gaze settling into hers.

"I remember perfectly," she said bluntly, meeting his stare with her own glare. She opened the door and strolled out into the harsh air without saying farewell.

.

3

CHAPTER THREE

"What's for dinner tonight?" Olivia inquired as Hans turned the key, opening the front door of his home. Swinging it open, he motioned for her to enter before locking the door behind them.

"You'll see," Hans grinned as he removed his coat and tossed it and his bag onto the side table.

"What's that?" Olivia inquired, pointing to a folder poking out of the front bag of the satchel.

"Just a report I've got to finish before tomorrow," he said. "I didn't want to delay our dinner so I brought it home."

"What's the report on?" She inquired, following him to the

kitchen. Though, to be honest, she wasn't very intrigued.
She hadn't done any poking about the workplace since her encounter with Harold and Cecilia the week before.
"It seems that there was an attempted break-out over the weekend. A jail transport was attacked on its way to Vught," Hans said, opening the fridge to get the fixings for supper. "Apparently some of the prisoners were family members of Dutch Resistance."
Lawrence is... Olivia froze, her heart sinking to her stomach at Hans's words. They had gone forward with a rescue effort. "Were they successful?" She inquired, attempting to keep her tone casual.
"Hardly," Hans shook his head. "There were only four of them so they never really stood a chance."
"What will happen to them?" She inquired, her heart hammering now. Why hadn't they received reinforcements? She had witnessed Calvin's desperation that night in the War Office, but she didn't expect them to be that desperate. They must have realized that going in alone would be suicide.
"I suppose they'll be taken to the camp with the rest of the prisoners," Hans said with a smirk.
"Do you think it's right?" She inquired, casting a peek at him. "Sending women and children to labor camps because of who

they're related to?"

"I don't have to think it's right..." He responded matter of factly. "It's an order."

"But surely you have an opinion," Olivia said, folding her arms over her chest.

"It doesn't matter what my opinion is," He shakes his head.

"It matters to me!" She answered, her tone rougher than she intended. "I'm sorry..." She exhaled.

"Don't be," Hans cut her off gently. He grabbed her forearms and unfolded them from over her chest, holding her hand in his while studying her countenance. "You've appeared distant for the last week... What is on your mind?"

"Do you ever wonder," she stopped and carefully chose her next words. "When it's all said and done, and this war is over, if we'll be on the right side of things?" She glanced up at him and instantly regretted her inquiry. He looked down at her with a wrinkled brow and a bewildered expression on his face. Of course, he had never considered that... Germany believed it was conducting a noble war. "I'm sure you think me treasonous," She laughed cruelly, attempting to remove her hand from his.

"No..." Hans grasped her hand before she could escape his grip. "I do not. In fact, the longer this battle lasts, the more I find myself asking the same question."

"How do you do this? How do you separate your duty from everything that is going wrong around you?" She asked seriously. She had been looking for an answer to that question for some time, and the process of distancing herself from her unpleasant reality was growing more difficult by the day. Harold had inquired whether she was capable of shutting herself off in order to do the task at hand. She considered herself to be... She believed she could keep her sentiments hidden in a distant corner of her heart. She was, however, living a lie, and the weight of that deception was becoming more apparent with each passing day... Feeling like an impostor in her own life.

So much so that even Hans, who had previously provided her with consolation, was becoming less of a comfort and more of a reminder of what she had attempted to divert herself from. After all, if he learned the truth, his feelings for her would undoubtedly fade.

"I love my country," Hans said, jolting her out of her thoughts. "And I don't want to see it broken ... Not again."

"When does love for one's country stop being enough?" She questioned, bringing her gaze back to his.

"I don't know," he said genuinely. "But what I do know," he said, stroking his fingers on her face.

"Is that this conflict, as horrific as it is, has brought you to me. And if it's the only good thing to come out of it all, I'll hold onto that."

Brushing back the hair on her face, he placed his lips tenderly to hers before breaking away for a little while. Her lips curled into a faint grin, and the weight in her chest shifted slightly for the first time in days.

"Let's go," Hans replied, holding her hand.

"Where are we going?" She inquired as he dragged her towards the front entrance. "What about dinner?"

"I've got another plan," he said, smiling over his shoulder. "You'll see."

4

CHAPTER FOUR

"Where are we going?" Olivia inquired, following after Hans, who was guiding her along the pavement with her hand.

"You'll see," he said, smiling at her. They went together for a few yards till they came to a little business on a street corner with the sign simply stating, 'Hoekmarkt'; Dutch for, 'Corner Market.' When they opened the door, a bell rang to mark their arrival. A chubby guy with a dirty white apron pushed open the kitchen door, a smile on his wide face.

"Captain Friedrich," the guy smiled, "a little late to be picking up your usual."

"Usual?" Olivia inquired, furrowing her brow.

"I come here for lunch most days," Hans said, smirking. "Mr. Baldwin here has the best roast beef in town."

"And who might this young lady be?" Mr. Baldwin inquired, raising an eyebrow at Hans.

"This is Olivia," he said, smiling.

"It's a pleasure to meet you," Olivia remarked, offering her hand to Mr. Baldwin.

"The pleasure is entirely mine," Mr. Baldwin said with a grin. "Any friend of Hans's is a friend of ours.

"Order whatever you want, as long as it's to go," Hans remarked.

"We're not eating here?" She inquired, giving him a skeptical look.

"This isn't our final destination," Hans said with a cheeky grin.

"Well, I suppose I'll take the usual then," She grinned, returning the paper menu Mr. Baldwin had handed her.
"Two roast beef sandwiches, then," Hans said with a sneer, returning his menu.
They waited while Mr. Baldwin made their order, drinking on the glass bottle cokes he had sneaked from the fridge. In less than fifteen minutes, he emerged from the kitchen with a brown paper bag. Hans took the bag, thanked him, and paid before moving toward the door.
"See you tomorrow for lunch," Hans said, jingling the bell as he pushed open the door.
"So where to now?" Olivia inquired after they had resumed strolling down the sidewalk. Hans provided no response other than a smile. "Let me guess," she said cynically, taking a drink from her coke. "Another surprise." They traveled a few more streets till they reached the front steps of the War Office. She saw Hans rummage in his pocket for his keys as she turned down the side street they frequented when Hans had to work late. "Why are we at the office?" She inquired after he had opened the backdoor and escorted her in.
"Come on," he said, smirking. She chuckled and followed him down the corridor to the familiar set of stairs that went to the top floor. She remained quiet as they mounted the stairs,

knowing just where they were heading.

"I know you loved this place," he added as they reached the top of the stairs. Smiling sweetly, he guided her into the center of the main room, which was decorated with the same familiar artwork as previously.

"And I also know that, even though this is home, it doesn't feel like much of one right now," he said. Taking a seat on the hardwood, he tapped the floor next him and motioned for her to sit.

She stooped down, smiling, and smoothed up her clothing before taking a seat near him.

Waiting patiently as he went to work unpacking their impromptu picnic, she peered about the room, her attention falling on the night sky just outside the window. The moon was a dazzling white tonight, and its light seemed to envelop the whole night sky as well as everything under it. It touched everything, and its warm colors blanketed the metropolis below and beyond.

"Do you miss your home?" She inquired, removing her gaze from the window to glance at Hans.

"I do," he nodded, setting her sandwich in front of her before unwrapping his. "I just hope I have one to return to when it's all said and done," he continued, his tone light, but his face revealed the slightest hint of tension. She nodded and unwrapped her sandwich as well.

"I'm sure you think I have a very obtuse outlook on things," Hans replied after they had sat in quiet for a bit. The sentence was unprompted, but she understood what he meant. He was alluding to the chat they had back at his residence.

"I think you have a job that forces you to," she remarked matter-of-factly, wiping her mouth with the back of her palm and wadding up the empty wrapper.

"Hmmm" Hans said, nodding in agreement.

"The military doesn't give you the opportunity to express your opinion on much, that's for sure."

"Especially when that opinion might contradict what they're doing," she said playfully, knowing full well how accurate that was.

"They would like us to perceive the world in black and white... And maybe once, at a time, I did," he said, leaning back and supporting himself on his hands. "But the longer this war drags on, the more I've started to see that the world is grayer than they'd like to believe." He glanced aside, as if lost in meditation.

Olivia observed him, observing his expression. He seemed tired, as if he was carrying something heavy. "I don't want you to think poorly of me," he added after a lengthy pause, keeping his eyes directed away from where she sat.

"I think you're a good man," she murmured, holding his hand. "A good man who finds himself in very difficult circumstances," she said, gently squeezing his hand. She knew he was in turmoil within... Agonizing over whether what you were doing was appropriate... If the goals justified the methods. Hans gazed at her; his eyes focused on her.

"What made you want to work for the War Office?" He inquired, as if considering the topic for the first time. "I mean, this is your house. Why work for those who took it from you?"

"This place hasn't been home for quite some time." She looked aside, her attention returning to the starry sky. "Not since I had my family with me. Grace is all I have right now; we are all either has. Working at the War Office was..." She trailed off, unable to find the appropriate term. "Safe... It was safe," she lied, a rush of remorse coursing through her chest. Taking the post had been the complete opposite of safe. Safe would have gotten on the ship to England. Safe would have meant leaving Holland for forever. She accepted the role out of selfishness... She hadn't recognized it until now, but that is exactly what it had been. Selfishness camouflaged as a moral desire for justice.

"Grace deserves to keep what little family she has left," she said, referring to herself rather than Hans.

"Why didn't you go to England too?" He asked. His inquiry was not accusatory, but she couldn't help but feel the shame tightening inside her chest.

"I don't know," she said, shaking her head. "I suppose I wasn't quite ready to move on." This was true. She had decided to remain since quitting would mean admitting defeat. Leaving had meant letting go, something she wasn't ready for.

"Well, I'm glad you didn't," Hans murmured, putting his palm over hers. "I'd very well be dead if you had," he continued, a tiny grin curling his lips.

She smiled back, and the weight on her chest shifted for the second time that night.

"Thank you," she said quietly. "For bringing me here again."

"Of course," he said, pressing his forehead to hers and gently brushing his lips against her own.

5

CHAPTER FIVE

"Hello, sir," Olivia said to the General as she entered the conference room for the daily security briefing. General Sinclair sat alone at the conference table, reviewing the day's agenda as he usually did before each meeting. He glanced up, a combination of astonishment and perplexity on his face as his gaze rested on her.

"My apologies, Ms. Carter," he murmured, rising to his feet. "But I'm afraid we won't be needing you this afternoon."

"Oh..." She blinked, releasing the chair she was ready to take away from the table. She took a step back and gazed up at him properly.
"I sent word to Mr. Mills ... I take it he didn't tell you," He presented the facts. He did not seem furious, yet his countenance was stiff nevertheless.
"No, sir," she said, shaking her head.
"I'm sorry for the misunderstanding," he replied with a compassionate grin.
"Sir," she hesitated, carefully considering her next words. "Have ... Have I done something wro-," She was interrupted by the sound of the door opening. Lieutenant Hayes entered the room, his eyes immediately meeting with Olivia's, and his lips curled into a grin at the sight of her. She glanced aside quickly, her attention fixed on the floor.
"I'll see you bright and early in the morning, Ms. Carter," General Sinclair said. His tone, although not dismissive, conveyed a sense of finality, indicating that their talk was ended, at least for now.
"Of course, sir," she said, without meeting his eyes. Swallowing down her feelings of fear and shame, she made her way to the door, trying to maintain a calm demeanor.

Taking a left down the corridor, she marched towards the restroom, almost breaking through the swinging door. She sat down on the toilet seat, locking the cubicle door behind her and running a hand through her hair to try to calm the rushing thoughts in her head.

Why had she been removed from the security briefings? Have they found who she actually is? Had Lawrence or the other Resistance members handed her up as part of a deal? It was unusual for the Third Reich to take a cautious approach to a possible danger... They would usually act first and then ask questions. If they had even the slightest suspicion that she was working with the enemy, she would have already been shot in the back of the head. Still, something was wrong... Perhaps they suspected her of something. She had no idea what they were keeping her away from; but why else would they be doing so?

She stood up, took a long breath, and slowly exhaled. Putting it out of her mind, she unlocked the stall, returned to the corridor, and sat down at her desk. She'd try her best to seem normal and go about her day as usual... She would accomplish her agenda for the morning and then go home. She was meeting Hans at seven p.m. for their dinner reservation, and she expected to hear a response then. Surely, he would have noticed her absence from the meeting and enquired as to why she had been excluded. She could rely on him to give her the truth, or at least on her capacity to detect if he was hiding anything from her.

***

Olivia looked down at her watch. It was quarter past seven, and she was still waiting outside the War Office's rear entrance. She and Hans had agreed to meet at the restaurant where they had a reservation, which was just a few streets away, but he had yet to emerge from the building. She opened the door and stepped inside, down the long corridor that led to Hans's office. She approached his door and knocked quietly before pulling it open. Hans sat at his desk, leaning over a stack of papers, his head raised up with a palm on each of his temples.

"Ahem," she cleared her throat. He glanced up, his brow furrowing in puzzlement, as if shocked to discover her standing in the doorway of his office.

"We were meant to meet for supper, at seven?" She responded inquisitively.

"Damn it," he said, staring at the clock on the wall and running an angry palm over his face. "I apologize... I lost track of time."

"What's going on?" She inquired, her brow furrowing slightly.

"The supply transports were ambushed last night," he said with a sigh, exaggerating the tired appearance he already had.

"By who?" She inquired, genuinely shocked. Despite knowing precisely who had carried out the ambush, Harold and Cecilia had failed to provide her with any information about when the operation would take place. She had known it would happen soon, but not this quickly.

"Brits..." He drifted off, finishing the tumbler of Scotch resting on his desk. "It seemed as if they were just sitting there waiting... They were on the trucks as soon as they reached the border."

"What did they do with the supplies?"

"They probably took what they could and burned the rest," he shrugged apathetically. "Those guys relied on those transports... If they had any prospect of making it through the winter, that's gone now." He shook his head, reaching for the bottle of Scotch.

Olivia looked at the bottle as he poured himself another drink. The black liquid that had almost reached the bottle's top earlier that week was now almost gone. He seems to have had a difficult evening.

"Are there no other relief efforts being made?" She inquired, partly looking for information, partly trying to discover a silver lining for him.

"There's nothing solid enough to be worth anything. Berlin is struggling to meet the Western front's supply requirements...

Much less deliver provisions to Stalingrad." He groaned and took a long drink from his glass.

"Will they surrender then?"

"That request was denied a week ago," he said dismissively.

"Denied?" She wrinkled her brow in perplexity. Why would Hitler turn down a proposal for surrender? Surely, he noticed the writing on the wall.

"The Führer denied General Paulus' request for surrender," Hans said, his tone rougher, though she couldn't tell whether he was irritated by her query or the response.

"So, Hitler would rather those men starve than admit defeat?" She inquired; her tone harsh despite her best efforts to conceal her displeasure. She was outraged by the idea of a nation abandoning its soldiers for murder in the sake of honor.

"I don't think you understand what surrendering would mean," he said, shaking his head. "It would not be like surrendering to the British or Americans... Those soldiers would not be treated with decency or respect, and they would not be transferred to some posh POW camp in Southampton." He went on, his brow furrowing in annoyance.

"This is a struggle with the Soviets... the same people who would sooner burn down their cities than let us conquer them. This is personal. Why do you believe they fought tooth and nail for

Stalingrad? Those guys would not make it out of the city. Those who were not tortured or executed would be transferred to a work camp in the heart of a Siberian wilderness."

Olivia found it strange that Hans thought the Soviets were cruel, especially given how much death and ruin his own people had caused. She pushed the notion aside and returned her focus to Hans. His eyes were red and inflamed, most likely from the quantity of alcohol he had drunk; the wrinkle in his forehead was deeper than when she first entered his office. Something else bothered him.

"There's something else," she continued, her brow furrowed in alarm. She awaited his reply.

"They knew those transports would be there... They were waiting for us," he said, shaking his head. "You don't get very fortunate. The only way they could have known the specific date, time, and place was if they had obtained it straight from the source," he said, his last words lingering in the air.

"You think there's a spy?" Olivia inquired, taking special effort to keep her voice steady despite her gut twisting into a tight knot.

"That's the only explanation," Hans said, shrugging and sighing in frustration. "Whether someone broke in and stole the information or is passing it from the inside, it's the only thing that makes sense."

"Is that why I was kept out of today's meeting?" Despite her best attempts to appear nonchalant, she offered a question that came out as overbearing.

"It wasn't just you," Hans shook his head, ignoring her apprehensive face. "General Sinclair is under strict orders from Berlin to eliminate anyone who isn't essential... including nonmilitary personnel," he continued with a sympathetic grin.

"To be honest, I wish you would've been there today," he said, his mood softening. "If I have to sit through another meeting with grown men talking over one another with no sense of direction I might go insane."

She smiled, and the sinking sensation in her stomach subsided somewhat.

"Anyway, it looks like I'll be pulling some late nights at the office for the foreseeable future," Hans moaned, pushed himself away from the desk and leaning back in his chair, motioning for her to come forward.

"Why's that?" She inquired, exiting the doorway where she had been standing and closed it behind her. Hans placed his arm around her waist, drawing her down into his lap. She wrapped an arm around his neck, leaned against his chest, and kissed his lips briefly.

"I've been assigned the task of locating the source of the leak," he said, resting a palm on her knee. "And ensuring it doesn't happen again."

She gulped as the pit of her stomach twisted into another tight knot. So, Hans was in charge of locating the mole. She sat on the lap of the guy charged with finding her true identity... The concept made her feel ill.

"I've been digging through case files all evening," Hans said, oblivious to the tension in her gaze. She looked at the mounds of files on his desktop, some of which dated back to the previous summer, before either of them had ever been at the War Office.

"What are you looking for exactly?"

"Clues," he answered. "A certain name that keeps coming up... A comparable event that may have occurred... It could be anything."

"Could it have been Dutch Resistance?" She inquired, catching him out of the corner of her eye.

"They've certainly got a reputable number of files to their name," he replied, pointing to the stack on his desk.

"But I don't believe they are behind it. This was too structured. Resistance generally comes strong and quick, with little consideration placed into the follow-through. That's why the Brits dislike working with them. Too much responsibility. If one of them became irresponsible and was apprehended, it might derail the whole plan."

Olivia recalled her interaction with Lawrence and the other Resistance members. That night, everyone in the War Office appeared emotional, particularly Calvin. And they definitely hadn't hesitated to launch an assault without assistance. She couldn't blame them, however. The memory of her sister being stolen had plagued her nightmares too many times to count, and she was confident that if she were in the same circumstances, she would do the same thing they had done, consequences be damned. Perhaps that is why Harold had been so stern in his warnings... Because he recognized the same reckless fire inside her that had led Calvin and the others to their doom.

"As much as I'd like you to stay right here for the rest of the night, I really should get back to work," Hans murmured, giving her knee a small squeeze and bringing her back to reality.

"Right," she said, clearing her throat. Bracing her hand on his shoulder, she rose to her feet. Hans stepped up, grabbing her hand before she walked away from him.

"I promise I'll make it up to you," he whispered, sliding an arm around her waist and bringing her close to him.

"How do you plan to do that?" She questioned, arching her brow.

A little grin formed on the corners of his lips. Leaning down, he kissed her, his lips leaving hers for a second before brushing over her jawline and neck. His hot breath on her ear sent shivers down her spine.

"You'll see."

6

CHAPTER SIX

"Olivia," Cecilia said, opening the front door wide for Olivia to enter. "Come in."

Giving Cecilia a tiny grin, she slid by her into the Winslows' entryway. She was worried about seeing Harold and Cecilia after her talk with Hans. She wanted to tell them everything. How did General Sinclair assume there was a spy? How Hans was appointed to lead the probe. When she found out, she wanted to rush to them right away, but she decided against it. To be honest, she'd been too terrified. She had almost been too terrified to attend their arranged meeting today, leaving almost a half hour earlier than normal to take a longer, less trafficked route home.

She was being paranoid... She knew that. However, the notion that the guy she had become so close to was now in charge of capturing her made her pulse race. That was why she needed to speak with the Winslows... She sought reassurance. I needed them to inform her that she was safe... At least as secure as an unknown Jewish operative spying on the Nazis could be.

"Olivia," Harold nodded, already situated in his normal chair in the sitting room, holding a tumbler of Scotch.

"I take it the ambush went according to plan," she added, not wanting to spend time on niceties.

"So, you've heard?" He raised his brow.

"It has everyone at The War Office in quite a fit," she said, taking a seat on the couch opposite from him.

"I would imagine so," he chuckled. "Rations and ammunition to sustain the Nazis another six months, with the twenty men delivering it all, were apprehended by Allied troops... Makes for quite the blunder," he said, lifting his glass in a faux toast.

"What are they saying in your meetings?" Cecilia inquired as she took a seat on the armchair next Harold.

"I wouldn't know," she responded, taking a long breath before proceeding. "I'm no longer invited to attend the security briefings."

"What do you mean?" Cecilia inquired, furrowing her brow.

"Apparently, non-military personnel are no longer considered essential to the higher-profile meetings," she said, keeping a careful eye on Harold and Cecilia's reactions. "General Sinclair received the orders from Berlin after the ambush and a handful of people, myself included, were removed."

"Well, I suppose that does throw a wrench in our plans," Harold shrugged. "But I can't claim we weren't expecting this. When something like this occurs, it's only natural that they tighten the reins a little. There are other methods to get information, however," he said, giving Olivia an insinuating glance.

"There's something else," she said, her lips drying. "They believe there is a spy... It's the only way to explain how the Allies knew about the supply transports," she said, as Harold and Cecilia exchanged shocked stares.

"What's being done about it?" Cecilia asked.

"Jo-," she started, then corrected herself. "Captain Fisher is in charge of the inquiry."

"Does he suspect you?" Cecilia said,

"No, I'm not sure... I-I don't think so." She stopped; her lips considerably dry than usual. She wasn't sure what she expected them to say once she delivered them the news. But she had been hoping for a little more support than she was now getting. "He certainly doesn't act like he thinks I'm the mole, but ... I can't be sure."

"Well, you need to be sure," Harold remarked, placing his Scotch glass on the side table.

"How can I?" She inquired, the edge in her voice clear now. "I'm sure he's just as capable of deceiving me as I am him."

"Is he keeping records?" Cecilia joined in.

"He had a large stack of paperwork on his desk... He said he was going through them one by one."

"So, he must be taking notes," Harold stated matter-of-factly, as if he had just revealed the solution to all of their problems. "Find them, and see what they say."

"He has no reason to suspect you," Cecilia remarked, offering Olivia a comforting gesture. "You are unassuming... That's what made you ideal for this position."

"No one suspects the pretty, little, Dutch girl," Harold said, almost patronizingly. "And they're not going to start now ... So long as you don't give them a reason to."

"Nevertheless," Cecilia interjected, "I don't believe it would be good for us to continue meeting like way... I believe we should postpone all meetings until alternate, less noticeable arrangements can be established," she said, turning to Harold for confirmation. He nodded, picking up his glass and took a longer draw than normal.

"What am I to do until then?" She didn't like the notion of being alone, with no safety net in case she needed one. As much as she wanted to think her bond with Hans would keep her safe, she couldn't be that gullible. If Hans, or anyone else, discovered the truth, she'd be done.

"Exactly what you're doing now," Harold said. "Get those notes and everything else you can, but keep it secure... Now is not the time to bring attention to oneself. We'll notify you when we can meet again."

"How will you get word to me if we won't be meeting?"

"Don't worry about that," he said, shaking his head.

"Well," Cecilia said, rising to her feet. "Let's not drag this out if we don't have to. You should get going."

"I'll walk you out," Harold said, rising to his feet as well.

"All right then," Cecilia shrugged, sharing a puzzled glance with Olivia. "We'll talk soon," she said, nodding and smiling reassuringly.

Olivia got to her feet and followed Harold out of the sitting room into the foyer. When he opened the front door, he moved aside and motioned for her to come forward. She complied, going outside into the harsh January air.

"I want to give you something," Harold remarked as they both went out onto the front porch, the front door closing securely behind them. She observed as he fiddled with something in his pocket before extending his hand, which was firmly gripping something within a closed fist. She extended her hand to take whatever he intended to offer her. He grabbed her hand with both of his, dropping whatever he was carrying into her palm. As he drew his hands away, her gaze landed on two tablets.

"What are they?" She inquired, although she assumed she knew precisely what the capsules, with their powdered white contents, were for.

"Every agent is issued two of these when they enter the service," he said matter-of-factly. "These are mine."

"I can't handle this... What if you need—"

"They fit inside this," he said, not letting her dispute. He reached into his pocket again and held out a little cylindrical tube that resembled a bullet. He unscrewed the lid, opened it, and grabbed the tablets from Olivia. He pushed them down into the tube, replaced the lid, and gave it to her.

"Cecilia would think I was nuts for giving you these... And God forbid you ever use them, but if you do..." He trailed off, as if looking for something to say.

"Well, a speedy death is better to some things. Do you understand? Keep it with you always."

She nodded. She turned the tube over in her fingers and inspected it. She'd never considered suicide, but Harold was correct. If anything happened, if she was caught, she could only pray for a swift, painless death.

"I know these last few weeks haven't been easy for you," Harold said, breaking the stillness and interrupting her thoughts. "But you've done well."

She gazed up at him. The severe attitude he so frequently wore seemed strained, as if it was battling for victory over the anxiety in his eyes. "Thank you," she said with a nod. He nodded, sliding his hands uncomfortably into his pockets.

"Get going... It's best not to dawdle out in the open like this," he murmured, his grave face returning. She nodded, sliding the tablets into her handbag before turning and descending the stairs.

"Olivia," Harold yelled as she stepped a few meters away. She glanced over her shoulder at him. "Be careful."

7

CHAPTER SEVEN

Olivia flipped the page, peeking over the top of the book she was reading. This was the seventh time she had remained late to sit with Hans while he worked on his report. The first night had been siOliviar to their typical nights spent working late at the workplace. They had spoken as Hans went through the ever-increasing stack of paperwork on his desk, taken a break for food and coffee, and called it a night by 8 p.m. However, with each passing night, the chats and pauses became shorter and shorter, until both had come to an end. She'd been sitting in her customary location, the armchair right across from Hans's, for over two hours, and he hadn't said anything to her despite her several efforts to start a conversation.

"As much as I like sitting with you while you work, wouldn't you say it's about time for a break?" She chimed, shutting the copy of 'Great Expectations' that Hans had given her for Christmas. "We could go pick up dinner-," She continued, but was cut off.

"I'm not hungry," Hans said firmly, his gaze fixed on the page he was reading.

"Well..." Olivia started, placing her book on the desk. "We could get some coffee... I am sure the café down the street is still operating. If we hurry–"

"You're free to leave if this isn't entertaining enough for you," he said sharply, his gaze flashing up to her.

"That's not what I meant..." She trailed off, surprised by his quick outburst.

"I'm sorry this isn't how you planned to spend your evening, but when I said I needed to work, I meant it," he snarled, his words flowing out with venom she hadn't heard from him before. "The door's there if you need it," he said, indicating toward the door before returning his focus to the paperwork on his desk.

Olivia brushed away the tears that burnt her eyes. Hans had never been upset with her, much alone raised his voice at her.

She fought back tears, altering her face to conceal the pain his words had caused. If he didn't want her there, that was OK. She'd depart.

She grabbed her book from the desk, then flung her purse and coat over her shoulder. She grasped the doorframe and peered over her shoulder at Hans. He was remained sitting, his gaze never leaving the pages in front of him. She looked at him for a time. His brows were wrinkled, causing the rest of his face to seem stressed. His eyes were heavy and bloodshot, despite the untouched tumbler of Scotch on the desk beside him. He seemed weary.

"I'll see you tomorrow then," she added, leaving the office when he didn't respond. She groaned as she proceeded down the long corridor to the War Office's rear door, putting her arms under her coat. She was almost halfway down the corridor when a hand grabbed her arm, causing her to swivel around to face the person who held it. Hans came before her, a contrite expression on his face, coat in hand.

"I'm sorry," he replied sincerely. "I didn't mean any of that."

"I know," she said, offering him a sympathetic grin.

"Come on," he said, nodding towards the door at the end of the hall as he put on his coat.

"But I thought-," she said, her brow furrowing in uncertainty.

"It can all wait until morning," he shook his head, wrapping an arm over her shoulders and giving her a little grin. She reciprocated his grin, wrapping an arm around his waist as they walked towards the entrance.

***

"Have you made any progress?" Olivia inquired, when she and Hans had returned to his place. Her mind had been distracted on their walk home from the workplace, with half of her time spent worried about Hans and the other half worrying about what would happen if he ever discovered the truth.

"I wish I could say so..." He yelled from the kitchen, where he was already getting the kettle ready for tea. "The truth is, I don't even know where to begin," he said, turning to face her as she entered the kitchen.

"You still don't think it could be someone who broke in?" She inquired nonchalantly, dropping her coat on one of the dining room chairs.

"No... No, it has to be someone from inside," he said, taking two glasses from the cabinet. "Who that someone is..." He finished with a sour 'Hmmm.'

"So, it could be anybody... It is also impossible to determine how long they have been in operation. For all we know, the guy who attempted to assassinate General Sinclair last year may have been the same."

"I thought the assassination attempt was carried out by the Resistance," she said, accepting the cup of tea Hans had prepared for her.

"That was the assumption, but no one was ever caught," he said with a laugh. "When I accepted this position, I thought I'd be updating a few out-of-date security protocols ... Not investigating a potential spy within the War Office," he said with a laugh.

"I'm sure General Sinclair wouldn't have put you in charge if he didn't think you could do it," she added, smiling reassuringly.

"Hmmm... You flatter me," He returned her grin, but it did not reach his eyes. "Honestly, I'm a little out of my depth," he said, shaking his head. "And as if that wasn't enough, we'll be getting a visit from Berlin."

"A visit?" She wrinkled her brow.

"As I'm sure you can imagine, the Führer wasn't thrilled to hear a supply transport had been intercepted behind German lines," Hans went on to say. "Berlin wants answers."

"When will they arrive?"

"Two weeks," he responded.

"So soon?"

"It would be sooner, but Thomas Evans is in Rome on official business at the moment," he said with a laugh.

"Thomas Evans?" She'd never heard that name before, but if he was being sent to Rome on behalf of the Führer, she assumed he was someone significant.

"Head of the Gestapo."

"The head of the Gestapo will be here?" She took a drink from her cup, attempting to conceal her astonishment. The prospect of the Gestapo snooping about the War Office made her stomach churn. However, the chief of the Gestapo said, "They want answers, and Evans is the best at getting them."

"Have you ever met him?" She inquired, taking another sip of tea.

"Thomas Evans?" he inquired. He shook his head and drank from his cup. "No ... He is not a military guy, at least not in the traditional sense."

"How so?" She inquired, setting her cup down on the counter.

"He's not enlisted," Hans explained. "His rank is more of a ... political one."

"I see," she replied, her thoughts racing as she attempted to grasp what he was telling her. "What will he do once he arrives?"

"I imagine he'll open an inquiry of his own," he remarked, taking his cup with him.
"Starting with this report, I have yet to finish," he remarked, removing the tiny folder from his backpack that he had carried with him from the workplace.
"If you need to work, please do," she said earnestly. As worried as this research made her, she felt awful about disturbing him. Furthermore, if Hans comes to his own judgment, Thomas Evans may accept his report without performing his own inquiry. "I don't want to distract you."
"I believe it's a little late for that," he remarked, placing the file onto the kitchen counter. He grabbed her waist and dragged her towards him. He relaxed into her, nuzzling his cheek against the crook of her neck and inhaling deeply before exhaling slowly. His breath sent a shiver down her spine, which got stronger when he brushed his lips across the flesh on her neck. "Besides, I think work can wait."
"I'm starving," she muttered, closing her eyes as he proceeded to kiss her neck and collarbone.
"So am I," he murmured against her ear, causing her cheeks to heat. Her breath caught in her throat as his fangs skimmed her earlobe and his hands pressed her body against his. She brought her arms up and wrapped them around his neck.

"Wha-what about dinner?" She asked half-heartedly.

With each brush of his lips across her flesh, her mind became foggy, with memories of the Gestapo and official inquiries fading. Cupping her bottom, he raised her off the ground and seated her on the kitchen counter.

"I think dinner can wait too; don't you think?" Hans answered, laying his hands on her thighs.

"I suppose it can," She grinned coyly and ran her fingers through the hair at the back of his neck. Wrapping her legs around his waist, she drew him closer, pushing her lips against his.

Hans lifted her from the counter and carried her out of the kitchen and down the hall to the bedroom. He pushed the door open with the toe of his boot and hauled her inside, dumping her upon the bed. She fell on the mattress with a thump, giggling as he unlaced his boots and leaped into the vacant space beside her, forcing her to bounce a few inches into the air. She rolled over on her side to face him. She smiled, running the back of her fingers up his face and returning her gaze to the blue eyes that stared at her caressing aside the hair that had slipped out of the pins that held them in place, he laid his palm on her face, his thumb barely caressing her lips.

"I love you," he added almost absentmindedly, shifting his attention from the point his thumb had been tracing to her eyes.

"I love you." And she did... with all of herself.

8

CHAPTER EIGHT

"Well, I have to say," Hans said, sliding onto his back. "This was certainly preferable to my original plans for tonight."

"You mean your original plans didn't include this?" Olivia smirked. She sat up, slipping her leg over his waist, and straddled him.

"Not quite," he said, matching her smirk. Sitting up, he grabbed her waist and pulled her against his chest.

"What a horrible oversight," she said, shaking her head in fake astonishment.

"Oh, believe me," he started. He leaned closer, running his hands up and down her back till their noses came into contact. "I know."

She mashed her lips against his in a brief kiss before drawing away. "You seem more like yourself now," she remarked, placing her forehead against his.

"How so?" He asked, trailing a path of kisses down her jaw and neck.

"You seemed so stressed before," she said, tipping her head up to give him access to her neck.

"I'm that transparent, huh?" Pulling aside to gaze at her, he slid a hand around her neck, his fingers tangled in her hair.

"It's the brows... They give you away," she replied, placing her finger into the gap between his eyebrows. "You get a little wrinkle right here."

"Well, what about now?" He inquired, bending back so she could inspect him well.

"Not a wrinkle in sight," she smiled, putting her arms around his neck. She closed her eyes as his lips touched hers, pushing her breast against his as they kissed. She drew away after a time, swinging her leg over to sit back on the bed.

"Where are you going?" He inquired, grasping her hand as she rose out of bed.

"If we don't eat now, we'll go to bed hungry," she said, picking up Hans's abandoned button-down off the floor and putting it on.

"Would that really be so bad?" He grinned.

"I'll be back," she said, smiling. She turned around, buttoned the shirt's center two buttons, and kissed him on the lips before exiting the room.

Her bare feet slapped on the floor as she moved down the hall to the kitchen. She was famished, but the time to make a proper meal had already passed. She opened the fridge and peeked inside, examining the milk and eggs on the shelves. She closed the fridge and opened the cupboard, sorting through the canned vegetables, sugar and flour sacks, and tea tins. She closed the cupboard after taking out the new loaf of bread Hans had picked up from the bakery the day before, as well as the jar of jam. She took a knife from the drawer, opened the jam, and cut two slices off the bread. She used the knife to spread jam on each piece of bread and placed them on a dish.

When she finished picking up the dishes, she turned to go when she saw something. The folder with Hans's report lay in the exact position where he had flung it. Her gaze returned to the folder when she cast a glance over her shoulder at the vacant corridor. She decided to take one final peek behind her before placing the dishes on the counter. She grabbed the folder and opened it cautiously, thumbing over the pages as silently as possible.

Each page featured a unique name written across the header. Lieutenant Hayes, Lieutenant Cooper, and Captain Becker... The report went on to provide full background and personal information for everyone who had attended the security briefings... except one. Olivia.

She closed the folder and put it back on the counter. She wrinkled her brow. Did he really not suspect her, or had he just not gotten around to creating a file for her? Looking down the hall, she shoved the thoughts aside. Now was not the time to be concerned about any of this. Hans had undoubtedly already wondered where she was... She'd have to figure all of this out later. Picking up the dishes off the counter, she turned and walked back down the hall.

9

CHAPTER NINE

"Alright," General Sinclair got to his feet, signifying the conclusion of the morning meeting. "I believe that's all for today."

Olivia stifled a yawn as she packed her typewriter and grabbed the pages of minutes she had recorded throughout the conference. Standing up, she walked towards the entrance, her eyes scouring the decreasing mass of uniforms for Hans. He'd undoubtedly be on his way to work by now, having spent every free moment working on his report.

Hans had been working nonstop, staying late every night and getting up early to come to the workplace before anybody else. She'd spent the most of the evenings sitting in the chair across from Hans's desk, but this week she'd begun going to bed early. She was exhausted, and not only from staying up late many nights in a row. She felt fatigued, and no matter how much she slept, she couldn't escape the sensation. Hans suspected she was on the verge of a cold, but she chalked it up to stress.

Hans's report had expanded tremendously in size since she had looked at it about two weeks ago, and she hadn't been able to get her hands on it since. She hadn't heard anything from Harold or Cecilia, despite their promises to deliver word quickly. She had considered dropping by once or twice, but decided against it. Besides, there was virtually no fresh information to send along save the upcoming visit from the chief of the Gestapo. That alone was sufficient cause to remain away, at least until Thomas Evans returned to Berlin.

"Ms. Carter," General Sinclair yelled out from behind her. She turned on her heel and confronted him. "A word?"

"Of course, sir," she said, returning to his position at the head of the meeting table.

"As I'm sure you know, Thomas Evans will be arriving this Friday," he said in a businesslike tone. "Mrs. Sinclair and I will entertain him for supper that night. I'd want Captain Friedrich and you to attend as well."

"Oh. I-uh... Okay," she answered hesitantly, surprised by the request. "Sir, I don't mean to sound ungrateful, but... Why me?" She inquired after a minute. "I'm sure there are plenty of other, more important, people with more interesting things to say."

"There will be plenty of time for Mr. Evans to talk policy and politics," General Sinclair said with a sly grin. "This is more of a ... domestic endeavor."

"I see," she said, nodding. "So, you want someone ordinary in attendance." The idea of eating supper with Thomas Evans did not set right with her, but she couldn't refuse. She'd have to smile and suffer it. Besides, when else would she have the chance to lunch with the leader of the Gestapo? It would be the finest, if not the only, opportunity to obtain knowledge she would never have had otherwise. After all, stiff lips tended to soften in congenial company, particularly when there was wine around.

"I was going to say someone unaffiliated with the government or military," he said with a laugh. "But, yes. Someone ordinary," He echoed her sentence.

"Does Captain Friedrich know yet?" She asked. It seemed unusual that General Sinclair would offer this invitation to her rather than Hans.

"I'll leave that to you," he said, smiling. "Cocktail hour starts at 5:30."

10

CHAPTER TEN

"That must be Mr. Evans," General Sinclair responded as a knock came at the front door. He stood up and headed into the foyer.

Hans had picked her up at 5:15, and they'd arrived to the Sinclair's house just in time for cocktail hour. A tall, slender lady named Mrs. Sinclair met them at the door.

Her face was narrow, and her high cheekbones, which had a tinge of rosiness from the rouge she'd applied, stood out against her alabaster skin. Her golden hair was flecked with silver streaks and put back in an attractive updo. A strand of pearls decorated her neck, which looked great with the navy-blue pencil dress she wore.

She was stunning, and Olivia wondered how old she was. Despite the gradual graying of her hair, she seemed no older than forty.

"Would you like another dear?" Mrs. Sinclair inquired, jolting Olivia out of her musings.

"Oh, yes, please," she said, looking down at the empty martini glass in her hands. "Thank you."

"Mr. Evans," she heard General Sinclair say from the door to the sitting room. "This is Captain Hans Friedrich, head of security."

"Captain Friedrich," She heard a heavy German accent, which she assumed was Thomas Evans's.

"Nice to meet you, sir," Hans said.

Turning around, she paused as her gaze rested on Mr. Evans. She had seen him before. I've seen those eyes before. She wouldn't be able to forget them. Those green eyes looking at her now were the identical ones that had peered over her father and brother's dead corpses after they had been shot, with Thomas Evans pulling the trigger. The sound of breaking glass brought her quickly back to reality. Looking down at her feet, she saw the martini glass she was carrying had fractured into multiple pieces across the floor.

"Are you alright?" Mrs. Sinclair inquired, caressing Olivia's arm.

"I'm so sorry!" She started, brushing off the sinking sensation in her stomach. "I-I...," she tried to explain, then trailed off. Everyone in the room, including Thomas Evans, was looking at her.

Mrs. Sinclair waved her off, saying, "Oh, it's all right." She grabbed the tea towel from the bar cart and started gathering up the shattered bits. "There's plenty more where that one came from," she assured her.

"And who might this be?" Thomas Evans asked.

"This is Olivia Carter," General Sinclair responded. "My typist and a friend of Captain Friedrich's."

"Carter," Mr. Mills repeated with a little curiosity. "So, you're from Holland, yes?"

"Yes, sir," she answered, focusing all of her attention on keeping the hand she had offered to him steady.

"Well," he said, grasping her hand. "It's a pleasure to meet you Ms. Carter."

"Likewise," she said, giving her best grin.

"Here you are, dear," Mrs. Sinclair offered her another Martini. "Fresh drink, just like fresh... Can I give you anything, Mr. Evans?"

"Whatever you have, Mrs. Sinclair," Mr. Evans said with a kind grin. "I'm not partial."

"Scotch it is then," She smiled. "Gunther, why don't the four of you go ahead and take a seat at the table, dinner won't be much longer." With that, she went into the kitchen.

"So," Hans said as everyone took their places at the table. "How long is your visit with us Mr. Evans?"

"Just long enough to write up a report, I'm afraid," Mr. Evans said, taking the glass of Scotch Mrs. Sinclair had handed him. "There's much work still to be done on the Eastern front, what with the situation in Stalingrad."

"What's being done to remedy that situation?" Hans inquired, spreading the tablecloth on his place setting as Mrs. Sinclair produced a gleaming, crystal dish filled with salad.

"There's concern that the recent surrender of the Sixth Army might instill some sort of morale in the Soviets," Mr. Evans said, nodding gratefully as Mrs. Sinclair replenished his salad dish.

"Possibly enough to result in the Red Army's assault into German territory... Given that the bulk of ghettos are located along the border, they must be removed promptly."
"What will you do with all the people?" Mrs. Sinclair inquired politely, taking her seat at the table after everyone else was served.
"Well, we certainly can't risk the Soviets coming in and liberating entire communities of undesirables," he grinned, as if it were a joke. "They'll be resettled at more centralized locations like Auschwitz or Treblinka,"
"Surely those camps don't have the capacity for such a large number of people," Hans said.
"Population control measures will undoubtedly have to be implemented," Mr. Mills said callously. "Those too young to work ... The old and sick..." He was distracted by the sound of chair legs scraping against hardwood as Olivia sprang swiftly to her feet.
"I'm sorry," she said quickly, smiling. "I'm afraid I don't feel good... If you will excuse me." With that, she turned and left the dining room.
"My apologies... I shouldn't be discussing such things in mixed company," she heard Mr. Evans remark after she had turned the

corner into the corridor. "I hope I didn't give the poor girl too much of a fright."

She shuffled down the hall, opened the bathroom door, and crept inside, pushing her back against the cold wood after she'd shut herself in. She fell to her knees over the toilet and vomited many times before dry heaving set in. Bracing herself on the toilet bowl, she pushed back against the door, bringing her knees to her chest. She let out a choking sob, tears stinging her eyes as she held her head in her hands.

It felt like there was a 100-pound weight on her chest. She could not breathe, move, or see. The bathroom walls seemed like they were about to swallow her up as her vision started to tunnel, her lungs crying for the oxygen her short, quick breathing was denying them of.

She needed to remain cool. She needed to calm her breathing down. She closed her eyes and sat up straight, pushing her index fingers into her temples. 'In through your nose, out through your mouth,' she reminded herself, the tingling feeling in her fingers lessening with each deep breath. Slowly, she opened her eyes and rose to her feet. Bracing herself against the bathroom counter, she looked at herself in the mirror, telling herself to remain calm as she wiped the wet tears that had yet to flow from her eyes. She took one final big breath, flushed the toilet, and washed her hands before swiftly leaving the bathroom.

"Are you alright?" Hans inquired, rising to his feet as she reentered the dining room.

"Yes, of course," she reassured them all with a grin. "I apologize. I am not sure what came over me." She sat down once Hans had pulled out her chair. "I just felt faint all of the sudden."

"Do eat something, dear," Mrs. Sinclair said urgently. "That is probably what it is. You have barely touched your plate."

"Yes," she said, faking a half-hearted grin. "That's probably it."

"Are you alright?" Hans inquired after they had said their goodbyes and left the Sinclair's.

"I'm fine," she said, nodding. "Just tired."

"Are you sure?" He pushed; his face wrinkled in a troubled expression. "You were either ghost white, or as green as the olive in your martini all evening."

"I'm sure," she assured him. "I just need a good night's rest is all."

"So, let's go home," he murmured, placing his arm around her waist as they went down the sidewalk to his vehicle.

"I believe I will remain at my apartment tonight... If that's alright," she added, taking a quick glimpse at his countenance.

"All right... I'll take you home then," He, said casually, obviously unconcerned with her choice to remain in different locations for the night. Something told her it upset him more than he let on. When they arrived to the vehicle, he opened the passenger door for her and closed it behind her before walking around to the driver's side.

"It's probably for the best," he added after getting inside the vehicle and starting it. "I should go to bed too... I have an early morning at the office."

"On a Saturday?" she inquired. "I thought you'd filed your report already?"

"I have," he said, nodding. "Mr. Evans, however, wants information on any attacks on German personnel in the recent six months. There are a few boxes of evidence that have been gathering dust in the archives, and General Sinclair wants me to classify them for him."

"I see," she murmured absentmindedly, staring out the window as they drove by the dimly lighted businesses of downtown, the street lights throwing a hazy glow over them through the fog.

"Are you sure you're alright?" She snapped out of her daze when she heard Hans inquire. He gently squeezed the hand that was on her lap. "You seem distant."

"I'm fine... Just-"

"Tired," He finished for her. He didn't seem persuaded, however.

"I promise," she said, nodding seriously. She gripped his hand by interlacing her fingers with his. It wasn't simply tiredness after a long week, however. Fortunately, Mr. Evans wasn't interested in a nightcap after dinner, so they were able to depart soon after eating. The awful sensation that was twisting her insides had not gone away, and she still felt the want to vomit up the little food she'd managed to gulp down that evening.

When she first saw Thomas Evans's piercing green eyes, she was transported back in time. The same horror and misery had swept over her, freezing her to the bone, exactly as on that balmy July day.

She had wanted to run... Run as far as she could away from the waves of anguish that were about to drown her. Away from the terrifying thought that she might meet the same end as her father and brother at the hands of the monster sitting across the table from her. That is what he was. A monster. Only a monster could casually - and callously - discuss killing thousands of innocent people over a salad course.

That was not it, was it? Coming face to face with the killer of her father and brother was unsettling, but it wasn't her only concern. She had been concerned by something for the greater part of that week, but she was only now admitting it to herself. The fatigue... Waves of nausea appeared out of nowhere... She tried to forget about it... She attempted to chalk it up to stress. But when her period didn't arrive by the end of the week, it proved what she had been denying... She urgently wanted it to be false. She was pregnant.

11

CHAPTER ELEVEN

"Olivia," Cecilia said breathlessly, answering the door after Olivia had repeatedly banged on it. Her forehead furrowed in quick alarm. "What are you doing here? Is everything alright?"

"I think I'm in trouble," was all she could say as her gut tightened into a thousand small knots. She'd been debating whether to pay a visit to the Winslows, and after getting little sleep and spending the most of her morning crouched over a toilet bowl, she'd finally decided to bite the bullet. Hans would be at work all day, so she'd have plenty of time to sneak across town to Harold and Cecilia's and return without having to justify her absence.

"Come in," Cecilia said, leading her inside. "Quickly." She closed the door behind them, taking a sideways peek at the street in front of the home.

"Is Harold here?" She inquired, allowing Cecilia to take her out of the foyer and into the comfortable sitting area where their meetings were conducted.

"No. Cecilia said, "He's at work."

"Good," she thought to herself. The notion of conveying the news to Cecilia was dreadful enough, but she was especially worried about Harold's response.

"Olivia, what is this about? Are you OK?" Cecilia inquired, casting a dubious glance her way.

"I'm pregnant," she murmured, her words sounding flatter and more matter-of-fact than she had meant. Cecilia breathed quickly and took a seat on the couch before speaking.

"How sure are you?" She inquired, patting the seat and motioned for her to sit down.

"My monthlies haven't arrived," she said, taking a seat next Cecilia.

"Did they come last month?"

"Yes," she nodded.

"There's still a chance you're just late," Cecilia said, her tone devoid of confidence.

"That's not it," Olivia said, shaking her head. "I know in my heart it's not."

"Do you have any idea when it might've happened?"

"I..." She glanced aside, ashamed. Truthfully, that might have happened many times during the previous month. She didn't want to acknowledge this to Cecilia. "I can't be sure."

"I see," Cecilia said, nodding.

"What am I going to do?" She inquired, the knot in her gut creeping up her throat, bringing a new surge of tears that seared her eyes with it. She bit her cheek, ignoring the sensation.

"Absolutely nothing," Cecilia said, shaking her head. She grabs Olivia's hand and gives her a comforting squeeze. "I know a doctor who is discreet. He will have everything we need to take care of it."

"An abortion?" Olivia inquired, clearly taken aback by the notion. She shook her head and took her hand out of Cecilia's. She'd seen the aftermath of abortions several times at her father's clinic... The glassy, empty eyes of the females who had made the choice - or had it made for them.

"It's not what you're thinking," Cecilia assured her. "You're probably just a month or two along... He will offer you something to help you get through it. It will automatically disappear with your monthly bills. Maybe a little more bleeding than normal, but nothing to worry about."

"No," She rose to her feet. "I ... I can't."

"You are not the first woman in your position to end up in a family situation, and you will not be the last. This is how it is handled."

"No..." She shook her head dejectedly. Cecilia looked at her, a mournful expression on her face.

"You love him, don't you?" She inquired after the room had become silent. Olivia turned away, unwilling to endure her scrutinizing eyes any longer.

"Oh Olivia..." Cecilia sighed. "I know you believe he feels the same way - and maybe he does - but the two of you don't even know one other... Not really. The fact is that he has fallen in love with a ghost, and you are a disillusioned concept of what may be if he understood the truth." She got to her feet and softly touched Olivia's arm. "He doesn't, however. And he never will."

"I know that," she murmured, sliding back onto the couch.

"I know what you're feeling-," Cecilia started, but she stopped her short.

"No, you don't... You and Harold have discussed everything about yourself... You had to."

"I know what it feels like to love someone..." Cecilia proceeded despite Olivia's interruption. "And I know what it's like to feel like a shell of yourself because you can't have them." She drew Olivia to her feet by grasping her hand. "It will take a few days to make preparations. I'll send word once I've spoken with the doctor," she responded, essentially ending the call.

Olivia nodded, feeling more than she had ever felt before. She wasn't sure what she had anticipated from Cecilia... Understanding? Perhaps someone could listen to her? She had not acquired any of those items, however. She shuffled out of the sitting room, turning to face the door.

"Olivia!" Cecilia yelled as she approached the front door. She peered over her shoulder at Cecilia, who was propped up against the foyer doorway. "I know it doesn't seem so now," she said, smiling sympathetically as she had previously. "But you will be okay again."

12

CHAPTER TWELVEE

Olivia strolled along the sidewalk, her home coming into view farther down the road. She wasn't sure how long she'd been walking. She'd been on autopilot since she stepped out of the Winslows' front door. She had not counted the number of turns or streets she had traversed. She'd just continued going and ended herself on the familiar cobblestone that her heels now clicked against.

During her encounter with Cecilia, she moved from afraid to furious to numb. Cecilia had been correct, of course. Even if

Olivia didn't want to accept it. She couldn't tell Hans about her pregnancy.

She had known it all along. But the finality of hearing it from someone else wounded worse than she had expected. It was silly for her to be mourning something she had never possessed in the first place. Cecilia had also been correct about it. The finest existence she could ever dream for with Hans was nothing more than a deluded fantasy she'd created in her imagination. She had allowed herself to think that the thought may be true... She allowed herself to fall in love with.

She shuffled up the front steps of her home, pulling her key from her pocketbook. After turning the key in the lock, her front door snapped open, and she went inside. She pulled her coat off and hung it, along with her handbag, on the hook beside the entrance. Turning around, she started in astonishment, her gaze resting on the stranger sat in her kitchen.

"Hans..." She trailed off, puzzled. He sat still at the kitchen table, elbows resting on his knees, gaze fixed on the flooring in a blank look. "What are you doing here?"

"Do you remember that German officer who was shot in the west village a few months ago?" He started, his eyes still following the wooden grooves in the floor. "Well," he proceeded without giving her a chance to respond. "I was looking back over the evidence when I found something." He glanced up at her for the first time since she stepped in the door. His stare was mournful and vacant. She took a hesitant step forward. Something was not right.

"Did you know the only thing found at the scene was a locket?" He pushed on. Holding up his left hand, which had been firmly clinched in a fist, he opened it, a glitter of gold catching Olivia's sight as a necklace chain slid out of his palm, dangling from the finger around which it was coiled. Her locket.

"This locket ... Which looks a lot like the one your mother gave you."

"Jos-," she started, her stomach tightening into an agonizing knot.

"I thought I was crazy for even thinking about it," he interrupted, rising to his feet. The deathly calm veneer he had maintained until now was starting to break. "So, I came here, but you weren't home," he said, setting the locket on the kitchen table. "I thought I'd have a quick look around ... find the locket ... prove my suspicions wrong."

"You went through my things?" She inquired, a lump developing in her throat.

"But I didn't discover a locket. Instead, I discovered this," he said without answering her inquiry. He reached behind him and took her revolver from the waistband of his jeans.

"Did you know this is a British Military issued revolver... and the same type of gun used to kill Officer Spencer," he added again, his tone deathly calm.

"Jos-," she attempted to say, but was stopped again.

"Officer Spencer," He clinched his teeth as he uttered her victim's name. "It was his name. The man you killed."

"Hans..."

"Who are you?" He asked.

"You know who I am," She swallowed the knot in her throat and stepped forward.

"No," he interrupted again. "I just assumed I did... So, I'll ask again: Who are you? Who are you?!" He let out a loud cry and pointed the gun at her.

"Olivia... Olivia Kensington," she stammered out, retreating involuntarily from his thunderous voice.

"You're Jewish?" He inquired, disbelievingly.

"Half Jewish... My mother was Dutch." She stopped, unsure how much to tell. She decided there was no need to hold back any longer. "Carter was her maiden name."

"Tell me," he said, his tone heavy with scorn, the rifle barrel still firmly aimed in her way. "How can a Jewish-Dutch girl become a British informant? I assume that's what you are, correct?"

"It's quite a long story," she replied, coming closer towards Hans. "So, either shoot me, and get it over with, or put the gun down."

"Go on," he yelled, almost throwing the rifle down on the kitchen table.

"My father and brother were not killed in a car accident," she said softly, taking in a long breath. "They were murdered by the Gestapo," she said, her voice ringing through the emptiness in the room. She breathed forcefully, bringing herself up to her full height before continuing.

"When Poland collapsed, we believed Holland would soon follow suit. When Holland was invaded, all working Jewish males were required to register. My sister and I didn't need to... At least not right now. My father was able to acquire paperwork for us using our mother's surname—"

"Forged papers," he interrupted.

"So," she went on. "When the rest of the Jewish people was required to register, we were exempt. We resided in the boarding house above the clinic, acting as orphans whom my father had taken in. No one asked any questions, and those who knew the truth knew not to say anything.

"That doesn't explain how you became a spy," he remarked, giving her a contemptuous stare.

"Everyone recognized my father... He was the top physician in the city. Everyone came to his clinic, including the Germans," she stated. "So, when the Jews were picked up and expelled, he was permitted to remain... I suppose they thought he was useful," she said, shaking her head.

"My father was aware that his worth was falling by the day. He knew it wouldn't be long before he and my brother were hauled off to a slum, leaving my sister and me behind. So... He made a bargain."

"What kind of deal?" He inquired, his brow furrowing with skepticism.

"In exchange for my and my sister's safe passage to England, he would spy on German officials who visited his office for treatment," she added, speaking fluently now that the knot in her throat had receded to her stomach.

"For over a year, everything ran just as planned. But then..." She hesitated, biting her cheek in an attempt to maintain a businesslike tone. "My father's British employer was uncovered. The Gestapo apprehended him and tortured him for information... I'm said he waited twenty-eight hours before revealing my father's identity... I suppose they meant that as some sort of consolation," she said angrily.

"They arrived at our door in less than an hour... My sister and I watched from above the clinic as our father and brother were led out into the street... They were pulled down onto their knees and shot in the back of the head." She described the events of that day robotically, attempting to distance herself from the agony it had caused.

"I knew we couldn't remain there, so we went to the safe home where we'd been told to go if anything like this ever happened. They maintained their word... We were each granted a ticket on a steam ship bound for London." She shook her head slightly, lost in thought.

"But I couldn't go... I couldn't go away and risk losing all my father had labored for. So, I remained and assumed my father's position... I had just gotten my assignment when you arrived at my door."

"Why didn't you kill me?" He asked plainly.

"I thought about it," she said, catching his eyes for the first time since she began speaking. "I could never bring myself to do it."

"Yet you can shoot a German officer and leave him to bleed out in an alley," he said accusingly.

"He attacked me!" She shot back, a combination of rage and anguish welling up within her. "He would've raped me and left me to bleed out in that alley!" He'd been there after it occurred. I saw the scrapes and bruises Officer Spencer had given her. How could he stand there and defend the guy he'd pushed her to denounce to police the night it happened?

"I didn't have a choice..." She added in a whisper, images of Officer Spencer's bloodied corpse rushing through her mind. She closed her eyes and pushed the thoughts away.

"I'm such a fool," Hans said, shaking his head.

"What?" She questioned, opening her eyes to fully look at him. His back was to her, and he had gone a few steps away.

"I fell in love with you... And the whole time it's been a game." He raked his fingers through his hair, his voice filled with contempt.

"No-" she protested, the lump returning to her throat.

"Then what has it been Olivia?" He roared and turned to face her.

"None of this was supposed to happen," she shook her head, tears welling in her eyes. "You were supposed to leave... I wasn't expected to see you again."

"But you did," he snapped back. And you've been using me for information ever since."
"At first, I was," she said. "But then-then something changed... Everything changed."
"Oh, spare me Olivia!" He shouted, shaking his head sharply. "Tell me... Did they instruct you to sleep with me, or was it totally your decision?"
"It wasn't like that!" She implored, wanting to make him understand. "I believed I could detach myself... I thought I could draw a boundary between my career and my affections for you."
"You should've gotten on that boat with your sister," he said, shaking his head and running his furious palm over his lips. "Christ, you should've gotten as far from this place as possible."
"I never meant to hurt you," she whispered gently, a single tear slipping down her face. She hastily wiped it away, tightening her teeth to avoid from breaking down completely.
"Go," he replied, his eyes returning to her. His eyes had become empty with indifference, replacing the wrath that had once filled them.
"What?" She inquired breathlessly.
"Go... leave," he repeated. "Go to your contact and inform them that you have been made... Tell them you want out; I don't care

what you say... Just make sure you get on the next ship out of Holland.

"Why are you doing this?"

"A life for a life," he said bluntly, avoiding to look at her. "And now that my debt to you is paid, I don't want to see you again."

With that, he marched passed her to the door.

"Hans," she said, quietly begging with him to turn and look at her. He hesitated at the entrance, twisting his head to the side, but his gaze did not meet hers. "When I said I had fallen in love with you," she said genuinely. "I meant it." They waited in quiet for what seemed like an eternity before Hans turned the knob and opened the door.

"Goodbye, Olivia," he muttered, closing the door behind him.

13

CHAPTER THIRTEEN

Olivia leaned against the sink bowl, splashing cold water on her face and looked in the mirror. Her swollen, inflamed eyes were surrounded by dark circles, and her typical rose complexion had faded to a pale, waxy one.

She'd spent the past day in bed, the events of the previous 24 hours still too unreal to understand. She had been forced to confront the fragility of her connection with Hans. A fragility she'd always been aware of instinctively, but had done her best to keep it out of her thoughts until now.

It had all occurred so quickly. Everything had been torn away in an instant, leaving her to pick up the pieces.

However, no fragments of her remained... She had unwittingly handed Hans every single bit that was left. She'd let her innocence plant a seed of hope in her heart. Hope for a different conclusion than the one that had been staring her right in the face all along. Hans would never love her, not for who she actually was. Their relationship was based on half-truths and deceit. How could she have allowed herself to hope that anything worthwhile might come of it?

She hadn't been able to bring herself to face the Winslows, particularly Harold. She needed time to digest, but she wasn't sure what good it had done. She stopped sobbing that night and fell asleep in the early hours of the morning. She would have to inform Harold and Cecilia today, however. They would be disappointed. Harold would shout. Cecilia would offer her a sympathetic look and claim she understood her feelings. She didn't, however. Cecilia would never realize how completely devastated she felt... She had been nursing a broken heart for far too long... Hans's brokenness had been repaired, but only temporarily.

She straightened her untidy hair with a comb and pinned it back. After one final look in the mirror, she returned down the hall to her bedroom. She took off yesterday's clothing, unlocked her closet, and picked out the first item she saw.

She put the green cloth over her head, buttoned up the front of the dress, and wore a white cardigan over it. She took her pocketbook and coat from the peg by the front door and went outside into the cold afternoon air. Squinting as her eyes acclimated to the brightness, she continued the usual drive to the Winslows' home.

She hadn't given any consideration to what she'd say when she arrived at the Winslow's door. Though she didn't think there was much to say. She had been constructed... They would want the details, of course, but nothing she could give them would erase the reality that it had ended. She'd be on the first ship to London before the week ended.

She had considered the probable consequences of her arrest for the rest of the SIS operatives in Holland, but she would be lying if she claimed she cared. Honestly, she didn't care about anything anymore. She had said that she believed in the cause. In the struggle for justice. Perhaps some of her did at first. If she were being honest, she hadn't remained to finish some noble objective. She had not been battling for the greater good... She had been striving for vengeance. She wanted to take everything from those who had stolen everything from her.

"Get off of me!" As she reached the corner into Winslow's street, she was startled awake by the sound of someone yelling. Looking up, her gaze landed on Harold, who was battling two cops attempting to detain him. One of the grey uniformed men raised his rifle and hit Harold in the back of the head, causing his body to go limp as they dragged him to the black Mercedes parked in front of the home.

"Please!" She overheard Cecilia exclaim as she jerked against the cop holding her. "Please, why are you doing this?" She continued to beg, convincingly portraying the innocent housewife.

Olivia was horrified as she realized what was going on. She had seen the grey uniforms before... Gestapo. Ducking behind a nearby house, she pushed her back against the cold brick, resisting the sinking sensation in her gut. She stayed stiff as a statue, stuck to the location, until she saw the black automobile drive by. Pushing herself from the wall, she almost raced back to her home.

***

She burst through the front door and flung her coat and luggage on the floor. Tears streamed from her eyes as she raced across the kitchen, her mind racing with a million emotions. It was over. It was over. She didn't think things could get much worse, but with Harold and Cecilia jailed, her final hope was cut off. There would be no ship and no way out. She was trapped,. stranded in a faraway nation she used to call home.

She was in a distant nation, surrounded by adversaries. How long would it take until the Winslows handed her up, or before the Gestapo linked the links on their own? She'd be caught... She was destined to share the same destiny as her father and brother.

Looking at the stack of paperwork she had taken home from the workplace the previous week, she flung them off the counter in rage, glass breaking on the hardwood as the flower vase that had been sitting on the counter crashed to the floor with them. She cried out, a choking sob smothering the scream she had planned to let out. She collapsed to the ground, leaned her back against the cabinets, ran her hands through her hair as tears streamed down her face.

She stared at the pile of paper and glass she'd made on the floor, and a little slip of paper caught her attention. Picking it up, she inspected it, her gaze following the cursive lettering on the page. It was an invitation to a banquet honoring Thomas Evans on Monday, February 15th. Tomorrow. She gritted her teeth and narrowed her gaze at the page. She crumpled the invitation and hurled it across the room. Thomas Evans had stolen everything from her and was going to pay for it.

14

CHAPTER FOURTEEN

Olivia halted at the double doors as she walked up the War Office's front steps. With the handbag slung over her shoulder, she drew the imprint of her pistol inside the bag. She slipped her opposite hand into the pocket of her dress and felt for the cylindrical tube containing the cyanide tablets Harold had given her. Turning it over with her fingertips, she traced the etching on the tube's surface, reviewing the plan in her brain one more time.

The ballroom would be packed with dinner guests eager to welcome Thomas Evans's arrival. He was going to suffer for what he had done to her and so many other innocent people. And she planned for him to pay tonight.

She pushed open the door and stepped inside, the gentle murmur of music in the distance filling her ears. She was going to murder him, and he would not see it coming. Of course, everyone else in attendance would be aware of what she had done... There was no way to disguise shooting someone at a dinner party... But that's exactly what the cyanide was for.

Her heels clicked on the floor as she walked down the corridor leading to the ballroom. Turning a corner, a hand grabbed her arm without warning and yanked her backwards violently.

"What are you doing here?" Hans growled and pushed her inside his office, slamming the door behind him.

She instantly clutched her purse and shoved it behind her. His gaze shifted from hers to the bag, narrowing in suspicion. Taking a step towards her, he grabbed the bag, taking it from her grip before she could draw away. Opening the clasp, he rummaged inside, his jaw clenched as he grabbed the pistol she'd hidden inside.

"Why are you here?" He asked again. Half-cocking the hammer, he opened the cylinder and removed each bullet from her revolver's cartridge. He put the rifle onto an armchair in the corner of the room after pocketing the ammo. "I told you to leave... Go to your folks and ask them to get you out!"

"I can't leave!" She snarled back at him with clinched teeth. "My handlers were arrested... I've got no one... There's nowhere to go... It's over."

"Why did you come here?" He looked at her curiously. She glanced away, her gaze fixed on a single shred of paper on Hans's desk... A piece of paper that was just like the one she had crushed yesterday. Hans's eyes followed hers and settled on the offer. "Olivia..." He trailed off, a look of awareness on his face as he started to connect the connections. His gaze shifted between the offer and the rifle, before returning to her.

"This is a suicide mission."

"He killed my father and brother," she said angrily, breaking all pretenses. "That was him! "He pulled the trigger."

"You can't really believe you'd even come remotely close to getting a shot off?" He shook his head, disbelieving. "The moment you pulled out that gun, they'd be on you before you could even cock the hammer."

"What if I had no intentions of leaving that room alive?" She inquired firmly, disregarding Hans's look of astonishment and grief at the inquiry.

"You think they'd kill you?" He scoffed. "They don't kill assassins," he said, shaking his head. "You would wish for death after the things they did."

"He's killed millions of innocent people," she said, dismissing his protestations. "He deserves to die!"

"That's not for you to decide," Hans said, his voice rising slightly.

"People like him took everything from me," she continued, echoing his tone.

"They haven't taken everything from you, Olivia," he said, his tone more frantic than furious. "You still have your life!"

"That's worthless to me now," she said, blinking and shaking her head regretfully.

"Would your sister say the same?" He inquired after the room had become silent. "Do you think your life means that little to Grace?" He pushed on, hoping she would glance at him. "You would deprive her of the only piece of family she has left? For what? Some self-righteous search for justice?"

"Grace lost her sister a long time ago," she said, despondent, tears scorching her eyes and threatening to spill over. "I am completely and totally alone," she shook her head, the sadness of her circumstance washing over her once again. "And I can't do this alone," she said in a hoarse murmur, clutching her tummy as a single tear fell down her face. Hans's gaze followed her hand, widening as awareness dawned on him.

"Olivia..." he started, his eyes returning to meet hers. "Are you..." He trailed off, unable to complete the inquiry.

She nodded and looked away, unwilling to meet his gaze.

"How long have you known?" He inquired breathlessly.

"Barely a week," she said, taking a glimpse at him. "I wanted to tell you..." She trailed off, pressing her eyes close to keep the tears at away. "But-," She was cut short when Hans's lips met hers, his arms closing around her in a tight hold. She melted beneath the familiar contact, locking eyes with him as he backed away.

"I'm sorry," she blurted out, tears streaming down her face. "I never meant for any of this to happen."

"I know," he said genuinely, cupping her face in his hands and wiping away the tears she had shed with his thumb. The phone suddenly rang, making both of them jump. "Wait here," He instructed, allowing her to answer the phone.

"Captain Friedrich," he said into the phone, after picking it up. "What?" He addressed the voice on the other end. "No... I haven't seen her," He answered, gazing Olivia's way. "Of course ...

I'll find her." He hung up the phone and turned to Olivia with a gloomy frown. "They know."

"What?" she questioned, reflexively backing away towards the door. This was it. They had worked out who she was.

"Olivia, wait," he whispered, extending out his hand to her. "Let me help you."

"How?"

"Meet me at the back entrance," he said, grabbing her hand in his. "Chances are that no one here has heard the news yet... There is still time to escape out. If you run into someone, act normally, but don't stay in the hallway for too long. I'll turn around and pick you up, and we'll work out a strategy from there."

"Hans, I don't know..." She trailed off, her heart racing.

"Do you trust me?" He inquired, looking into her eyes attentively.

She paused for a time, considering his question.

"I do," she said eventually.

"Then I'll see you in ten minutes." Picking up the revolver he'd left on the chair, he retrieved the rounds he'd stashed in his pocket and reloaded the chamber, offering her bag to her, the gun disguised within.

"Ten minutes," she said, taking the bag from him before moving toward the door.

She departed his office and turned down the corridor leading to the backdoor. She walked as slowly and carefully as she could, suppressing her impulse to bolt as quickly as possible. Finally, after what felt like ages, she reached the rear door.

Looking over her shoulder one final time, she pulled it open, letting in the cold night air.

"Ms. Carter," a voice yelled from behind her as she took a few steps outdoors... A familiar voice... from the person she'd least expected to see. She turned on her heel and faced Lieutenant Hayes. He stood a few meters away from her, a happy look on his face. She breathed hard, trying to match his grin.

"Hello, Lieutenant," she said, waving in his way.

"Leaving the party so soon?" He questioned, taking a few steps toward her.

"I'm afraid I'm not feeling well," she said sweetly, ignoring the thudding sound of her heartbeat in her ears. He did not respond, but made another deliberate stride towards her. "It was lovely to see you," she lied, taking a step back. "I really should be going, though," she said, giving him one more brief grin before turning on her heel.

She had traveled a few yards when a hand gripped over her lips and an arm wrapped around her waist, securing her against the body they belonged to. She kicked and struggled, attempting to extricate herself from Lieutenant Hayes's grip. Suddenly, a searing agony went through her skull, and her body fell limp in his arms as darkness enveloped her.

15

CHAPTER FIFTEEN

"Ah," Olivia heard someone remark, "You're awake."

"Whe- Where am I?" She inquired, her eyes fluttering open and straining as they acclimated to the dazzling brilliance of the light. Her head was aching, and her eyesight was still fuzzy from whatever damage she'd sustained. "Wha-What happened?" She inquired, attempting to identify the last thing she recalled. Why was her head aching so much? As she attempted to move her hand to her temple, she noticed for the first time that she was shackled.

She blinked her eyes to focus and gazed about, taking in her surroundings. She was in the midst of a tiny cinderblock room. A solitary fluorescent light flickered above her, creating a shadow in the remote corners of the room. Lieutenant Hayes sat on the other side of the table from her.

"Tell me, Ms. Carter," he said, resting his joined hands on the table and leaning forward. "How does a Jewish girl from Holland become an informant for British intelligence?" He hesitated, a knowing smile forming on the edges of his lips. "Or should I call you Ms. Kensington?"

"I don't know what you're talking about," she said, shaking her head. He knew. How did he know? Had whomever contacted Hans also informed Lieutenant Hayes? She swallowed the sinking sensation in her belly and tried to maintain a neutral appearance.

"Hmmm... Of course, you don't," he grinned, rising to his feet. "Two British agents were picked up yesterday evening and brought in for questioning," he continued, strolling around the table. "After nearly twenty-seven hours, it seems... Harold, is it?" He inquired, paying particular attention to her emotions when her handler's name came up. "Couldn't take another moment of his precious Cecilia being tortured," he went on to say. "So, he gave you up instead."

He pulled the chair back, his hands on the armrests, and stood straight in front of Olivia. "I will ask you again... How does a Jewish girl from Holland get involved with the British SIS?" He inquired, leaning down and laying his hands on the chair's armrests.

"You appear to have all the answers. Why aren't you asking me?" She responded, removing all pretense of innocence. He knew who she was. There was no denying it anymore. He drew back and smacked her hard across the face, her head swinging to the side as his palm made contact with her cheek. Blinking back the tears that had gathered in her eyes, she stared at him, unwilling to reveal any weakness.

"You know," he said, "I knew there was something off about you." He brought his hand up and touched a finger over her bruised face, causing her to grimace. "I never would've thought you were the mole though." He dropped his hand and put it on her knee, gently dragging it up her thigh, causing the hemline of her dress to rise.

"You're a coward," She spat, pulling her leg away from his contact.

"How's that?" He grinned and grabbed her inner thigh tightly, keeping it in place.

"You think you're so manly... Doing all of this while I'm tied up and unable to fight back," she muttered with clenched teeth.

Standing up straight, his grin grew.

He took his knife from its sheath and circled around to the back of her chair, violently grasping her wrists. She felt the ropes that had tied her relax as they were severed, dropping to the floor.

"Go ahead," he murmured, stepping behind her. "Fight back."

She slowly got to her feet and turned around to face him. He was observing her with a pleased grin on his face. She looked between him and the door, considering her choices. She could run... She had no idea where she was or how many German officers were waiting for her on the other side of the door. She could fight... Attempt to grab the revolver from the holster on his hip... Or maybe the knife?

"I'm waiting," he said, putting his palms out to the side as if to say, 'Come and get me.' He seemed to like it. She took a deep breath to quiet her pounding pulse and tried to think straight. Those drugs... Her thoughts went to the tube containing the two cyanide pills Harold had handed her... She had been carrying a tube in her pocket when she visited the War Office earlier that night. She pushed her fingers into the pockets of her dress and felt about for the chilly metal of the tube.

"Looking for this?" Lieutenant Hayes's sarcastic voice summoned. She glanced up, her gut tightening with fear as her gaze shifted to the gleaming thing he held between his index and middle fingers.

The pills!

"Your dear friend Cecilia had one just like this," he said, rolling it over in his fingers. He unscrewed the top and dumped the tube's contents onto his hand. "They caught her trying to take them," he said, holding up the capsules. "Too bad she wasn't successful," he said, dropping them to the ground. "She would've had a much more dignified death."

He stepped on them and crushed the tablets, leaving a little clump of white dust as the last vestige of her hope for a way out. He took a step closer to her, wiping away the powder with his boot. She pushed the chair in between them at him and dashed for the door.

She'd just taken a few steps when a hand grabbed her hair and yanked her backward. She yelped in agony as she was hurled to the ground, the wind rushing out of her lungs as she landed on the pavement with a bang.

"Good try," Lieutenant Hayes said cynically. He reared back abruptly, the toe of his boot contacting her ribcage. She yelled out, but only a little gasp escaped her lips, her lungs still empty from having the breath knocked out. Rolling over, she held her abdomen, gasping for oxygen as another hit landed on her stomach.

"Not so tough now, are we?" He jeered, his evil smirk clear in his tone. He crouched down and grabbed a fistful of her hair, pulling her to her feet. She reached up and clutched his hand, attempting to wrench it away as he dragged her. She shoved her forward and crashed against the table.

Turning to face him, she moved away, skirting around the table to create as much space between them as possible. Her throat clenched as she watched him, and her heart raced within her chest. He was observing her, his smile bigger than usual as he approached her slowly. As he approached, she backpedaled away from him. This was not an ordinary questioning. This was personal... Revenge for her rejection of him.

"You're just angry," she shouted out, fighting back the terror that tried to overwhelm her. "You're angry because I do not want you... I never wanted you!" She continued on, her back against the wall behind her. He had worked his way around the table, reducing the gap between them agonizingly slowly. He was flirting with her...

"I don't really care what you do or don't want," he joked, taking a few steps closer. She moved sideways into the wall, attempting to create more distance between them. She wanted more time to think about anything... anything.

Pushing herself from the wall, she moved to the other side of the room.

He grabbed her and pushed her back into the cinderblock, the agony in her ribs radiating throughout her body. She tilted her head, her chest heaving against his as he moved in closer. "I can't tell you how long I've wanted to do this," He whispered into her ear, grasping her chin firmly and yanking her head around to look at him.

She pushed him with all she had, but he stayed glued to the place, the wicked sneer on his lips coming up once again. Gripping her hips with his free hand, he pulled them back, keeping her against the wall.

"You disgust me," she said with clinched teeth. She spit in his face while looking up at him.

"You smug little bitch," he yelled at her, releasing her chin and wiping away the spit on his face. Grabbing a fistful of hair, he dragged her forward, pushing her against the table. She struggled and kicked against him as he grasped her waist and rolled her over so her stomach was flat on the table.

"You think you're too good for me," he said, his tone shifting from humor to wrath. He grabbed the hem of her dress and pulled it up, separating her legs with his knee. "We'll see how high and mighty you are after I finish with you," he mocked, fidgeting with his jeans buckle.

"Get off me!" She shouted and reached behind her in a desperate effort to push him away.

"Lieutenant Hayes," a familiar voice said from the door. "If you'd be so kind as to release the prisoner."

"Well, isn't it your lucky day," Lieutenant Hayes replied sarcastically, releasing her waist and straightening his pants. "Come to take a turn?" He inquired, shifting his gaze to Hans, who was still waiting in the doorway. "Though," he continued, seizing Olivia's arm and dragging her off the table. "I suppose you've had several turns, haven't you?"

"I've come to interrogate the prisoner," Hans said matter-of-factly.

"Are you sure that's such a good idea?" Lieutenant Hayes inquired, pressing her against him and twisting her arm behind her back. "Given the nature of your relationship?" He drew her closer as he looked her over. "Besides... We were just getting to the fun part, weren't we?" He jeered at her ear.

Olivia pulled her eyes tight, tears threatening to fall if she stared at Hans any longer. He'd betrayed her. Had lied to her. And she had believed him. Had thought he wanted to assist her... He believed he still loved her.

"That's enough," Hans said sternly.

"As the chief of security, I am in charge of interrogations until the Gestapo arrives. Thank you for your assistance, but you are free to go," He continued, moving to the side to make space for Lieutenant Hayes to depart through the door.

"Yes, Captain," Lieutenant Hayes said sarcastically. Dragging Olivia along with him, he thrust her forward, Hans grabbing her into his chest as Lieutenant Hayes walked out the door.

Olivia spit, "Don't touch me," as the door closed behind the Lieutenant. She strained against Hans's chest, attempting to extricate herself from his clutches.

"Stop," he murmured quietly, tightening his grip on her. "Stop it," he said more strongly, holding her shoulders.

"You lied to me!" She sobbed, her eyes burning and tears threatening to fall. "You said you'd help me! This was your plan all along!" She pushed him, slapping his chest violently.

"Listen to me!" He spoke through clinched teeth. He grabbed her forearms and pushed them against his chest, firmly keeping them in place. "I didn't lie to you," he said quietly. "I didn't realize Lieutenant Hayes knew your actual identity... I didn't realize he would be at the rear entrance... I had no idea any of this would happen," he said, looking honestly into her eyes. "I'd want to assist you... Please allow me to assist you."

"You can't help me," She shook her head, a single tear running down her face.

"Yes, I can," he answered, brushing away the tear and resting his palm on her face. She sank into his hug, shutting her eyes tight so that no more tears fell.

"Do you trust me?" He inquired, placing his forehead to hers. She nodded. "Then I need you to listen to me," he replied, drawing back to properly look at her. She opened her eyes and gazed up at him. "Don't give them anything, do you understand?" He started. "The moment they think they've gotten what they want out of you, you're of no use anymore." He reached down and put his palm on her stomach. "Not a word of this," he murmured quietly. "They'll only use it against you."

"I'm afraid," she said quietly, another tear slipping down her face. She felt afraid... No, not of dying, but of what was going to happen to her before she did... What was going to happen to both of them before she did. She grasped her tummy, her ribs still throbbing from Lieutenant Hayes's boot, her thoughts turning to the unborn child she carried inside.

"I know you are," he whispered, throwing his arms around her and laying his chin on the top of her head. I need you to be strong. I'm going to find out way to get you out of here, I vow.

16

CHAPTER SIXTEEN

Olivia sat at the table; knees drawn up to her chest. Hans had left the room over an hour ago, and she had been alone ever since. Her mind had raced with a million things the instant he walked out the door. How long would she be imprisoned in this little room? Will Hans be successful in getting her out of here? Will Lieutenant Hayes return to complete what he started? How soon would the Gestapo arrive?

The door creaked open, immediately jolting her out of her thoughts. Hans walked inside with a file in one hand and a tape recorder in the other, closing the door behind him. She stood up, expecting him to speak.

"I'm here to conduct your interview," He stated, pointing to the chair she had quickly risen from. "Please, sit."

Sitting down, she waited for him to cross the room and take a seat in the chair across from her. He put the file in front of him and set the recorder beside it.

"Before I turn this tape on, I want to be perfectly clear," he said. Leaning forward, he rested his elbows on the table. "I have a role to perform, and so do you. Do you understand?"

She nodded. They both had to play this game properly if they were going to make it out alive. Hans nodded and pressed play on the recorder.

"State your name," he said bluntly, opening the folder.

"Olivia Kensington," she answered.

"How old are you?"

"Twenty-two."

"Where are you from?"

"Den Haag."

"And where are you employed?"

"The German War Office."

"How do you know Harold Winslow, and Cecilia Hereford?"

"I don't," she lied.

"That's not what Captain Winslow had to say," he insisted.

"What did he have to say?"

"He told us you're the mole who has been passing information from the War Office to British Intelligence," he said matter-of-factly.

"I don't know what he's talking about," she said, shaking her head.

"Is it true you secured forged papers and have been living under the alias Olivia Carter?" He inquired, completely changing the topic of the discussion.

She hesitated and reluctantly replied him. "Yes."

"And is it true your father also operated as a spy for the SIS, and worked in close proximity with Captain Winslow?"

"I don't know." She knew it was all for show, but she was becoming agitated still. "He wasn't very open about his interactions with the British... Captain Winslow may have known my father.

"So," Hans said, skeptically. "You expect us to believe Captain Winslow fabricated the entire story, and decided to use an unassuming girl whom he's never met, and whose father he may or may not have worked with, as a scapegoat?"

"Men say a lot of things while being tortured," she said.

"True," he shrugged. "But the stories they tell often have a thread of truth to them."

"Well, his doesn't."

"Stop lying," he snarled through tight teeth, thumping his fist on the table. She startled at the unexpected shout.

"Captain Friedrich," a voice said from the doorway. Olivia's gaze shifted to the entryway, where two guys in dark grey uniforms waited.

"Can I help you?" Hans inquired, rising to his feet.

"S.S. Watson," the guy up front introduced himself. He was tall and powerful, with brilliant blonde hair peeking out the edges of his cap. "And this is S.S. Weston," he continued, nodding to the guy next him. S.S. Weston was a few inches shorter than Watson, but he could easily tower above Olivia by a foot. His hair was a deeper blonde, his eyes were a deep green, and he was looking straight at her. She averted her gaze, focusing her attention on the table while they continued to speak.

"I didn't think the Gestapo would arrive so quickly," Hans said as he approached the two policemen.

"We were told we needed to come right away," Watson said, accepting Hans's handshake. "Thank you, Captain, for getting things started, but I believe we'll take it from here."

"Of course," Hans said.

"Weston," S.S. Watson motioned towards Olivia. "Escort Ms. Kensington to a holding cell while I speak with the Captain."

With a nod, S.S. Weston approached her.

She did not resist, allowing him to take her out of the room and down a poorly lighted corridor. As he approached the end of the corridor, he opened a door and brought her inside. The room was the same as the one they had just left, with the exception of a bed in the far corner and a toilet in the other. He closed the door behind them and leaned against the wall, pulling an apple from his pocket.

"Are you hungry?" S.S. Weston inquired, holding out an apple. He took out his knife, chopped a bit, and held it out for Olivia to accept. "Take it," he said, pointing to his extended hand. She reluctantly grabbed it and ate it. She was famished after not eating for over 24 hours.

"You know, I've seen this happen before," he said, taking a mouthful. "A young, misguided girl gets in over her head because of the mistakes of someone else," he said with a laugh. "I get it." After finishing the apple, he lifted himself from the wall and dumped the core in the garbage before turning to face her.

"Just tell me whatever you know, and I can make all of this go away," he added mockingly. He attempted to influence her... Encourage her to let her defenses down. "You can trust me."

"I don't know anything," she said, shaking her head. He smiled sweetly at her, studying every detail of her face.

"That looks pretty bad," he replied, pointing to the bruise on her face where Lieutenant Hayes had struck her. "Did Captain Friedrich do that to you?"

"No," she said swiftly.

"So pretty," he stated matter-of-factly. He raised his hand and gently touched her face with the back of his finger. She flinched backward automatically, keeping her gaze fixed on his. "I'd hate to resort to less civilized methods to get what I want," he replied, locking his gaze on hers.

"I told you," she stepped back. "I don't know anything."

"Don't lie to me," he said, shaking his head. His face was serene and even pleasant. He stepped back, unbuttoned his uniform coat, and took it off. He folded it carefully and meticulously before placing it over the back of one of the chairs in the room. He pushed his button-down sleeves up to his elbows and unbuckled his belt, sliding it from the loops of his slacks. He approached her, looping the belt over his hand.

"I really don't want to mess up this lovely face," he whispered, brushing his fingers across her cheek again. "So, I'll ask you one more time before we start... What do you know?"

"I don't know anything, I swear." As she returned his gaze, tears filled her eyes. He gave out an impatient sigh, as if he was dreading what was going to happen.

He grabbed her arm and dragged her from the wall toward the middle of the room. He struck without warning, the belt connecting with her shoulder blade. She yelped in agony and fell to the ground. Rolling over, she raised her hands in self-defense, just as another punch struck her forearm.

"Please! Stop," she implored.

"I will. Once you tell me what I want to know," he said gently. He did not seem furious, like Lieutenant Hayes had. He was calm and calculated, as if he had done it a million times before.

"I don't know anything!" She yelled. She raised her knees to her chest and held her head in her arms, attempting to shield herself.

"More lies," he said matter-of-factly. Swinging the belt, he lashed her across her legs and then her arm.

"Tell me the truth Olivia." After a few more swings, he stepped back to assess his work.

She squinted through the tears that had filled her eyes, taking a peek at him. He was staring down at her with the belt still in his grasp. His gaze was bland, devoid of emotion as he watched her. She slowly lifted herself off the floor and got up on unsteady legs.

Her whole body hurt, her arms and legs covered in crimson stripes from the pounding she'd received. S.S. Weston smirked as he watched her try to rise.

"You're a tough little thing," he said, his sneer expanding. "We'll change that."

17

CHAPTER SEVENTEEN

"Get up." Olivia was woken from the slumber that had finally overcome her, her eyes flickering into focus as they fluttered open. The springs groaned under her as she moved over on the small mattress she'd snuggled up on, still dizzy and bewildered from being jolted awake so quickly. Her whole body hurt, every muscle aching from the multiple beatings she'd received during the previous 36 hours.

She wiped away the black crust her mascara had left under her eyes and stared down at the smudges on the backs of her palms. She didn't need a mirror to realize she looked terrible.

She was still dressed in the same clothing she had worn almost two days before, and the little makeup that hadn't been tears off was smeared down her cheeks. She winced as she forced herself into a sitting posture, her tight muscles reactivating. S.S. Weston stood over her, arms folded anxiously.

"Come on, let's go," He urged, taking her arm and pushing her to her feet.

"Where are we going?" She inquired, but didn't oppose as he drew her towards the door.

"Someone wants to see you," he said casually.

"Who?"

"You're quite inquisitive this morning," he replied with frustrated sarcasm. "You'll see," he said, before she could ask any more questions. She followed in silence as S.S. Weston led her down the hallway, faltering every few feet as she struggled to keep up with his rapid speed. His firm grasp on her arm kept her steady as they moved down the corridor to a familiar door. It was the room she'd been assigned when she initially arrived. S.S. Weston opened the door and pushed her inside.

"Here she is, sir," he remarked as the door closed behind them. Her pulse chilled as she followed S.S. Weston's gaze to a guy sitting at the table. Thomas Evans.

"Thank you, S.S. Weston," Mr. Evans grinned and nodded. S.S. Weston nodded again before heading for the door and departing.

"Hello, Ms. Kensington," he said once they were alone. "Please sit." He motioned to the chair across the table from him.

"I'd rather not," she said coldly.

"My apologies," he said, his cheerful manner unwavering. "I see you interpreted my kindness as a recommendation... It was not. Have a seat. His grin faded as he indicated to the chair again. She reluctantly crossed the room and drew the chair from the table, without taking her gaze away from him. "We're both well aware of your situation," he said after she was seated. "And I hear you've been making things tougher on yourself with your disobedience. This might all be fairly simple... If you tell us all we want to know."

"So, you can kill me after you get what you want?"

"Hmmm," he laughed. His eyes met hers, boring holes in them as he inspected her. She gazed back stubbornly, without saying anything. "When you first came here," He eventually spoke. "I'm sure S.S. Weston said he could make things better for you... That he could make all of this go away if you only answered his questions," he grinned.

"You were correct not to believe him. That was a lie. You see, the fact is that you will not get out of this alive. But you are aware of this, right?" He inquired, smirking. "That explains why you've been so quiet... It's your sole remaining negotiating chip, and it's not very good."

"I would disagree," she said.

"There are far worse things than death, Ms. Kensington," he grinned, leaning forward and resting his elbows on the table. "All of which, despite what you might think, you have yet to experience," He became quiet, his eyes studying her face for something... probably dread, she assumed. She gazed at him blankly, not allowing him the pleasure of terrifying her.

"Now, although you may not be able to choose your destination, you do have control over the route you take to get there. It might be a swift, respectable route or a lengthy, terrible one. Is there a clear understanding?"

"Crystal."

"Let's begin then, shall we?" He started by clasping his hands together on the table. "Why don't you tell me what you were doing in the War Office the night before last? You clearly weren't dressed for a dinner." He stopped, his gaze traveling down her physique, assessing her attire. "So, I can only assume your purpose for being there was something else."

"I was there to kill you," she said matter-of-factly.

"Hmmm... Were you now?" He chuckled. She gazed back at him, without responding. "That's quite a bold move for the British," he said, arching his brow. "Sending in an inexperienced, naive girl, to carry out an assassination."

"I was acting alone."

"You went rogue then?" He gave her an inquisitive glance. "Tell me... What makes me so odious to you that you'd give up everything to see me die? We had only just met, after all."

"We've met before."

"Have we?"

"In a way, yes," she said. "I knew exactly who you were the moment I saw your face."

"Please," he said, shrugging. "Enlighten me."

"There was a doctor and his son," she said calmly, tightening and unclenching her fists under the table. "You've murdered them... They were dragged out into the street and shot."

"You need to be more explicit than that. I've murdered a lot of people," he said, amused.

"They were Jewish and spies for the British," she said. He needed to remember. How could you not recall shooting two individuals in the back of the head? "Hmmm... Still not ringing any bells, I'm afraid." It was all a game to him. A fun little game.

"It was my father and brother," she said, clenching her teeth. She could feel her rage mounting. She loathed him... She hated him with all she had.

"So, you wanted vengeance for your family," he said patronizingly. "How terribly uninteresting ... I expected more from you."

"You murdered them," she continued, her tone increasing significantly.

"I executed enemies of the state," he said dismissively.

"What caused them to become enemies? Their espionage or their ethnicity?" She shot back, her cheeks becoming red with rage.

"I suppose both," he said, smirking.

"You disgust me," she said, shaking her head.

"You're not the first person to say that to me, and you won't be the last."

"You're a monster!" She spat, the chair skidding noisily over the concrete floor as she hastily sprang to her feet.

"Finally... something but brazen indifference. Now we're getting someplace."

"We're getting nowhere," she remarked between clenched teeth. He'd been teasing her... Trying to make her upset in the hopes that she would make a mistake and reveal something. And it had worked. Maybe not as well as he'd wanted, but it worked.
"We'll see," he said, smiling wickedly at her. He had gotten under her skin just enough to break her determination to remain quiet, and he knew it. She would not let that happen again.
She spun on her heel and headed for the exit. Mr. Evans did not try to stop her as she grasped the knob and twisted it. Jerking the door open, her torso collided with the tall frame of S.S. Weston, who had, of course, been standing guard at the entryway.
"Trying to make a run for it?" Weston questioned, holding her arms. "I thought you were smarter than that."
"It's okay," Mr. Evans said, waving his hand disinterestedly. "We're finished here... See you soon, Ms. Kensington," he replied, his evilly lovely grin resurfacing.
"When you reach your destination."

18

CHAPTER EIGHTEEN

It had been a week since her appointment with Thomas Evans, and the interrogations had become more harsh with each passing day. Every morning, she was dragged out of bed and taken to the same little, cinderblock chamber. If S.S. Watson was waiting for her, she knew it was going to be a long day. S.S. Weston did, however, lead some of the sessions. Those days were not as awful. He hadn't hit her since their initial meeting, and his interrogations were far gentler than his counterpart's.

She knew that was all part of the game they were playing with her, attempting to break her down. It was the classic "good cop, bad cop" routine.

Weston would accompany her to the chamber, Watson would torture her for information, and Weston would return to fetch her, tending to Watson's new wounds once they were back in her cell. She understood precisely what they were doing, yet the heavier Watson's beatings became, the more she craved Weston's deceptively reassuring touch afterwards.

Pulling her knees up to her chest, she slid onto her side on the cot, facing the wall. She had no clue what time it was, but dawn must have been arriving quickly. Staring at the cinderblock, she traced the grooves in the cement with her gaze, attempting to divert herself from the day ahead of her.

Wiping tears from her eyes, she took a long breath, her ribs throbbing as her lungs expanded. She needed to preserve her determination... Stay strong and wait for Hans. However, as time passed, she began to worry whether he would ever return for her. She'd had to fight the impulse to give up many times in the previous week. She'd wanted to tell them what she knew many times so that it could end. She couldn't do it, however. She trusted Hans... She needed to... It was the last thread of hope she had.

"Time to get up," S.S. Weston said as the cell door cracked open.

Olivia sat up, knees still securely hugged to her chest, wiping away one last stray tear.

"Let's go," he replied, seizing her arm and lifting her from the bed. She let him take her out of the room, her bare feet rubbing against the concrete floor as he took her down the corridor. After passing the familiar chamber where the interrogations were conducted, they continued on, heading down a path Olivia had never been down before.

"Where are we going?" She inquired as they took another corner.

"To the showers," Weston said matter-of-factly.

"Showers?" Her eyebrows furrowed.

"You haven't washed in over a week," He observed, leading her along. "You're starting to smell."

Her cheeks reddened. If she smelled as bad as she felt, she definitely needed a shower. She hadn't showered since the morning of her abduction. Despite her shame, she was relieved to take a shower. Not only did she want to become clean, but she also hoped that S.S. Weston would interrogate her today and she wouldn't have to face S.S. Watson.

Weston opened a door at the end of the corridor and brought her inside. It was a small, tiled room with no shower curtains and many shower heads along the walls. There was a bench to the side with a bar of soap, a towel, and a stack of freshly cleaned garments on it.

"Alright," Weston responded, releasing her arm. He took a step back, putting his back against the wall, after closing the door behind him.

"You're not going to leave?" She asked.

"And let you hang yourself from the shower head?" He raised an eyebrow and nodded towards the towel. "I'm staying right here," he said, shaking his head.

"I'm not showering in front of you," she protested vehemently. She had not considered suicide, but Weston stood there still, indicating that it had been tried before.

"Either you take your clothes off or I'll do it for you," he said matter-of-factly. She gave him a skeptical expression. Surely, he didn't expect her to strip nude in front of him.

"At least turn around," she added, requesting rather than commanding.

"Fine," he said, sighing after briefly contemplating her plea. "You have three minutes." He crossed his arms and looked away from her.

She quickly unfastened her dress and took it off, kicking it aside as it struck the floor. Discarding her underwear, she grabbed for the knob and cranked it, ice cold water bursting out of the shower head above her. She gasped, the chilly water snatching her breath away as it touched her skin.

Submerging herself beneath the chilly stream, she grabbed the bar of soap and lathered her hair and body with it, washing it off rapidly.

Turning the water off, she grabbed the towel and brushed herself off, wringing out her sopping wet hair with it before dumping it on the ground. Turning her attention to the garments arranged neatly on the bench, she took up the camisole and matching slip and slipped them on, the white fabric a dramatic contrast to the bruises that dotted her flesh, all at varying states of healing.

"Alright... time's up," Weston remarked. "I hope you're decent" He added as he turned around. His gaze moved down her figure, ending at her stomach. She followed his eyes to her bare tummy where the camisole hadn't covered. Yanking the cloth, the rest of the way down, she turned her back to him.

"You're pregnant."

"I don't know what you're talking about," She shook off his allegation, snatching the cream colored, cotton garment off the bench.

"Oh yeah?" He replied, seizing her arm and twisting her around to face him. "Then what's this?" Grabbing the hem of the camisole, he pushed it up, displaying the little lump that had just beginning to emerge from her tummy.

"Stop," She complained. Yanking her arm from his hold, she turned her back to him, tugging the cloth back down over her stomach. Slipping her arms inside the dress, she started to work buttoning up the front, ignoring the sensation of Weston's gazing gaze against her back.

"Who have you told?" He inquired after a lengthy minute of stillness.

"No one," She, said bluntly.

"Who's the father?"

"I don't know," She lied.

"Hmmm," He snickered. "That's a lie. You want me to think you've opened your legs for so many guys that you don't know who the father is, but you won't even take a shower in front of me?"

She bit her teeth at the rude statement. Turning on her heel, she sprang back to smack him. Catching her wrist before her hand could make contact, he dragged her forward, their noses almost touching.

"Did I hit a nerve?"

Glaring up at him, she wrenched her arm out of his clutches, and turned around.

"Is it that captain from the War Office?" He pressed.

"Go to hell," She yelled back, buttoning the final fastening on her dress.

"It is, isn't it?" He continued. "Captain Friedrich," He mentioned Hans's name. "I'd heard the two of you were sweet on each other," He pushed on, evident to the fact he was flustering her. "Does he know?"

"No," She lied.

"Probably for the best," He shrugged. "Wouldn't want to complicate things."

"No," She agreed firmly. "We wouldn't."

"Was it an accident, or part of your plan?"

"My plan?" She turned to face him, an impoverished expression on her face. Did he truly believe she'd gotten pregnant on purpose... Did it to lure Hans into giving her additional information. "A baby isn't a bargaining chip."

"It certainly can be," He shrugged. "If a man is naive enough to allow it."

"I'm ready to go," She responded, dismissing his statement. Dropping the topic, he grabbed for her arm to accompany her out. "I can manage on my own," She murmured, recoiling from his embrace.

"By all means then," He opened the door, nodding to the left. "This way." She walked alongside him; his hand placed softly against her back instead of securely around her arm as he guided her back down the corridor.

"Where are we going now?" She inquired after they'd passed the questioning room, and her cell.

"S.S. Watson will be questioning you somewhere different today," he said, bringing her down another hallway she'd never been down before.

Her blood turned cold at the sound of Watson's name. She stopped in place, the rage she'd held minutes before evaporating into sheer dread.

"No," She shook her head, pulling away from Weston. She wanted to leave... To turn and sprint back down the passage as quickly as she could. He swung around to face her, caught aback by her unexpected disobedience.

"Come on," He murmured grabbing for her arm. She moved back again, out of his grasp. She was afraid and it showed all over her face... She was confident of it. She didn't care however... Didn't care whether S.S. Weston noticed the dread in her eyes.

She couldn't bear another session with Watson... She hadn't understood exactly how much she couldn't tolerate it until now.

"Don't be stupid," He advised. Lunging at her, he seized her arm, pushing her forward violently.

"No," She pulled against him. "Please."

"Stop," he proceeded to push her forward, unperturbed by her pleas.

"Please don't leave me with him," She implored. She didn't care how desperate she sounded. She couldn't go back to S.S. Watson... She couldn't. "Please," She delivered one more desperate appeal as they reached their destination. She was grasping his arm strongly now, willing him not to go.

"I'll be back to get you," he murmured, his stern visage wavering for a single second as he peered into her eyes. Averting his eyes from hers, he resumed his frigid manner and opened the door. Pushing her inside, he slammed the door in her face.

"Have a seat Ms. Kensington," S.S. Watson yelled behind her. "I've got something new in store for you today."

19

CHAPTER NINETEEN

Olivia inhaled slowly, pushing back the horror that had seized her minutes before. She couldn't allow Watson to see her that way... She would not offer him pleasure. Her expression contorted into a defiant indifference, she looked over her shoulder, her gaze locked with his.

"I said have a seat," he repeated the command. She turned to face him; her feet firmly planted. He tightened his teeth with irritation. This was the same song and dance they performed every time. She would ignore his commands, pressing his buttons until he yelled at her. She was aware that she was making things tougher for herself, but she refused to lie down and surrender to him.

She would not give him that. Whatever he got from her, he'd have to remove with force. He unbuckled his belt and slid it off. Crossing the room, he seized her hair and slung her against the wall, her head striking the cinderblock with a thump, leaving a tiny cut on her temple. She blinked; her eyesight clouded with small, little dots as blood flowed from the incision. He grabbed her shoulder and twisted her around, pressing the front of her body against the wall.

"I'm growing increasingly tired of your disobedience," he growled into her ear. He grabbed her hands and dragged them behind her back. He grabbed the belt and wrapped it over her wrists, cinching it tight. After he had restrained her, he removed her off the wall and walked her across the room to the chair. He shoved her down into a sitting posture and looped a large rope around each ankle, binding them to the chair legs.

Looking down at the huge tub of water beside the chair, she wiped back tears that burned her eyes. Her head was pounding from the hit she had just taken, yet she could still think well enough to know precisely what Watson had planned for her. He was about to waterboard her.

Swallowing the fresh surge of horror that had rushed over her, she turned from the tub to S.S. Watson. He was watching her, looking for any flaws in the serenity she was attempting to project. She looked up at him stubbornly.

"Let's get started then, shall we?" He said, disregarding her disapproving face. "What information did you provide to SIS during your time at The War Office? I assume you know what this is?" When she did not respond to his original query, he focused his attention to the tub of water. She gazed at him and refused to recognize him. "Do you know how it works... waterboarding?"

"I have an idea," she said bluntly.

"It seems like you are drowning. As if you were about to die... You won't, however." He smiled, pulling up his uniform sleeves. "I can do it as many times as I want without killing you... Now, answer my question."

"Go to hell," she snapped back. He smacked her across the face, causing her head to jerk to the side. He grabbed a clump of her hair and yanked her head back, extending it over the back of the chair.

"Why don't I demonstrate?" He took a sopping wet towel out of the water and put it over her face, holding it securely at the back of her head.

"Mmmm!" She attempted to scream, but the taut cloth blocked away the sound. She struggled against her bindings as he held her down. Suddenly, water rushed her face, up her nose, and down her throat.

She attempted to scream, but no sound came out. Her nose, eyes, throat, and whole body burned. And then, just as swiftly as it began, it ended. S.S. Watson withdrew the towel from her face as she leaned forward, coughing and wheezing, struggling for breath after being suddenly denied of it.

"What about now?" He scowled at her. "Or should we go again?" When he wrapped the towel over her head, more water rushed into her mouth and up her nose as he poured it on her face. She fought for oxygen as he removed the towel again, spitting out the water she'd coughed up. "Ready to answer questions now?" He jeered at her, grasping her hair and forcing her head back to face him.

"Fu-fuck you," she said between panting gasps. His mouth clinched in rage. He had assumed she would break... It was evident on his face... And the fact that she hadn't already incensed him. He removed the knife from his pocket and cut the cords that had shackled her ankles. He grabbed her by the hair, pushed her onto her knees, and submerged her head into the tub of water. She pushed against him, pushing against the belt that still bound her hands. Was he intending to murder her or drown her? He yanked her head back up and dragged her body into his.

"You will break," he muttered to her ear. "I promise you."

She took a big breath immediately before being pushed back under the water. Her head was aching, and her eyesight became fuzzy. He drew her back above water, giving her barely a few seconds of reprieve before plunging her back under. Her lungs burnt from a lack of oxygen. She felt like she was about to pass out. He drew her up, her body growing limp against his, her eyelids fluttering shut as drowsiness threatened to overwhelm her.

Olivia opened her eyes, head hammering. She was resting on the cot in her cell, her hair still moist from the agony S.S. Watson had inflicted on her.

"You're awake," she heard someone say from the other side of the room. She glanced up, and her gaze fell on S.S. Weston. He approached her and pulled up a chair by her bed. He sat down and motioned for her to sit up, which she did. He tilted her head up by her chin and checked the cut on her temple.

"This would all be so much easier for you, if you'd just submit," he said, pressing his fingers on the wound. She flinched back, wincing. She watched as he removed gauze and antiseptic from the tiny first aid box he had taken with him.

"You think I can't see what you're doing?" She spoke icily.

"What do you mean?" He wrinkled his brow as he applied some of the antiseptic on the gauze.

"This whole routine of yours isn't lost on me," she continued, her tone colder. "You haven't lifted your hand to me since my first day here... Letting him do all the dirty work, while you swoop in to pick up the pieces once he's finished," she said, shaking her head. She was outraged with herself. She'd sought solace in the one place she could find it, despite the fact that she knew it was all a lie.

"You are attempting to acquire my trust... That I'll confide in you, or at the very least, let my guard down and slip up," she went on. "We both know it could just as easily be you beating me everyday, and you wouldn't lose a bit of sleep at night if it were," she said with a grin. This was true. Weston could have easily drowned her earlier today, with S.S. Watson currently caring to her wounds. They each had a role to play in this cat and mouse game, and they both did it very well. He looked at her, weighing her words.

"You're a lot smarter than they've given you credit for," He added after a lengthy pause. He reached up and wiped antiseptic-soaked gauze over the wound on her skull.

"What are you doing?" She recoiled at his contact. "I told you... I know why you're doing this."

"This still requires attention," he said simply, continuing to treat her wound. She did not complain, allowing him to thoroughly clean the wound.

"You said your father and brother were killed by Thomas Evans," He continued after they had sat quietly for a time.

"Yes."

"And you saw it happen?" He inquired, placing the antiseptic and gauze back in the first aid bag.

"Yes," she said, nodding. What was he getting at? This had nothing to do with the requested information.

"Why stay? Why not get out?"

"I was angry."

"Angry?"

"Angry that everything had been taken from me by people like you," she said coldly.

"You should've run." He had not intended it as a threat. As ridiculous as it sounds, his response seemed genuine.

"It's too late for that now," she answered grimly.

"Yes... I suppose it is."

20

CHAPTERTWENTY

"Time to get up," S.S. Weston's voice said, as a hand grabbed Olivia's arm and yanked her from the cot where she'd been sleeping. She wiped the fatigue from her eyes and followed S.S. Weston towards the door.

"Where are we going?"

"An old friend wants to see you."

"An old friend?" She wrinkled her brow, her thoughts instantly turning to Hans. She hadn't heard from him since the first day she arrived in this dreadful place, and despite her desire to cling on to the sliver of hope she still had, she was starting to believe she wouldn't.

She was taken out of her thoughts as the door to the questioning room opened. Her gaze rested on a tall, broad-shouldered guy sat at the table, his jet-black hair streaked with gray.

General Sinclair's gaze caught hers as the door banged shut behind her.

"Hello, Ms. Carter," he said politely. She looked at him, blinking in bewilderment. What was he doing here? "Please, have a seat," he urged, pointing to the chair across from him. Without saying anything, she crossed the room and sat down.

"I'm sorry for how you're being treated," General Sinclair said genuinely. "What the Gestapo does is a nasty business," he said, looking at the marks on her arms.

"Sir, if I can be honest," she said, folding her arms over her chest to conceal the blue and purple markings. "Why are you here?"

"I knew there was something about you from the moment we first met," he said nonchalantly. "I knew you were different... special," he grinned gently to himself. "I suppose what I've come here to ask you is, why?"

"Why?" She wrinkled her brow.

"From what I've heard, you had several opportunities to run... To leave the continent totally," he said, resting his elbows on the table and leaning forward. "Yet you stayed... Why?"

"I felt obligated to stay," she said matter-of-factly.

"An obligation?"

"Yes..." She trailed off, her eyes falling from his. "I suppose you think me ignorant and naive."

"On the contrary," he said, shaking his head. "I believe you're really brilliant... You'd have to be to go into a room full of high-ranking German commanders and mislead everyone all day, including yourself," he grinned. "The decision you made took a lot of courage."

"What?" Her gaze shifted up to his.

"We're all fighting for what we believe in here, Ms. Carter," he said calmly. "Just because you're fighting for the other side doesn't make your choice to remain and fight any less heroic... I only wish we'd been on the same side," he said with a sorrowful grin.

"Sir, I want you to know..." She trailed off, searching for the appropriate words. "I want you to know that it was never personal. You were really kind to me, and despite the circumstances, I was always grateful for it."

"I know," he said, nodding.

"I suppose this is goodbye then," She felt a sense of remorse in her breast, but she had no idea why. At the end of the day, General Sinclair remained the enemy, no matter how polite he had been to her. After all, he didn't know her genuine identity.

"I suppose it is Ms. Carter," he said, nodding. He rose to his feet after pushing his chair back.

"It's Kensington, sir," she corrected softly.

"I know," he said, smiling. "Oh, I almost forgot," He went into his pocket and took out a little, folded slip of paper. "Captain Friedrich asked me to give this to you." He stretched the paper towards her. She looked at it cautiously before accepting it. She flipped it over with her hands but did not open it. "In spite of himself, he cares for you," General Sinclair observed as she perused the letter.

"I never meant to hurt him," she whispered, more to herself than to General Sinclair, her gaze fixed on the message.

"I understand... However, jobs like these have a tendency to leave collateral damage in their wake," He remarked, giving her a knowing look. She caught his eyes and nodded in accord. "Goodbye, Ms. Carter," he said, smiling. She watched as he spun on his heel and vanished, the door thudding shut behind him.

She returned her attention to the paper in her hand, unfolded it, and started reading.

"Olivia, I'm writing to ask you one more thing before we say goodbye. If you ever had any feelings for me, tell them what they want to know. I can't bear the notion of how much anguish you must be going through any longer. End this for both of us."

She gulped down the nauseating sensation in her throat. Was this a trick? The handwriting seemed to be Hans's, but it may have been falsified. She paused for a moment before continuing to read.

"I want you to know that I care about you, despite all of the pain you have given me. Suffering, after all, is more powerful than any other teaching tool, and it has taught me to realize what your heart used to be. It has bent and broken me."

"But, I hope, into a better shape," She concluded a passage from Great Expectations. Hans had quoted practically word for word from the letter. She wrinkled her brow, attempting to make sense of his statements. He had undoubtedly written it. The allusion to the book he had given her for Christmas cemented this in her mind. But why?

She read the message many times before folding it and slipping it under the waistband of her slip.

Smoothing her dress back down, she walked towards the exit, her gaze catching S.S. Weston's as she opened the door.

"About time," he muttered, pushing his palm to her back. She went alongside him in silence as he took her down the corridor to her cell. Her mind was racing with million ideas. Hans had clearly instructed her not to tell them anything. Why is there such a dramatic change? What did he mean by 'before we say goodbye?' Did he have a strategy to get her out of here? If he did, she didn't see how giving away the one thing that was keeping her alive at the time could be part of the plan.

Despite the enigmatic phrasing of the message, her instincts urged her to trust him... So, she would.

She would trust him.

21

CHAPTER TWENTY-ONE

"Time to get up," S.S. Weston's voice said, startling Olivia awake like it did every morning.

She'd gotten much less sleep than normal previous night, unable to stop the rushing thoughts in her brain. She had studied the paragraphs of Hans's letter many times, looking for any hidden message she had missed. She hadn't discovered any, however. I'm not sure what his strategy was, or even if he had one. She had made one decision, however. Today, she would abandon the item she had been hanging to for the previous two weeks. She'd give them everything they wanted.

S.S. Weston grasped her arm, dragging her from her fetal posture to her feet. He rushed her to the door.

"Wait," she whispered, pulling her arm away from his clutches.

"Let's go," he replied, exasperated. He grabbed her arm more firmly this time and drew her forward. "Come on, Olivia... Don't make it any harder."

"I'll tell you," she blurted.

"What?" S.S. Weston gazed down at her.

"I'll tell you everything," she said, taking in a long breath. "Just don't take me back to him."

"Wait here," he replied, letting go of her arm and turning on his heel.

She stood still, waiting. What would happen if she handed up the knowledge she held? Would Weston allow S.S. Watson to torment her anyway? Will she be transported someplace else or remain here? She had little time to consider the alternatives, since S.S. Weston returned after a short pause.

"Sit down," he said, pulling up the metal chair that was usually placed next to the entrance. She sat on the mattress and watched him seat in the chair opposite her. He pulled a tiny, black box from his coat pocket and turned a switch, causing a red light to flicker on the front of the box. Tossing it, the tape recorder fell with a bang on the mattress near her. "You said you'd tell me everything," he added, gesturing to the recorder. "Go ahead."

And she did. She told him everything. What had happened to her father and brother, and who had killed them? Thomas Evans. How she became a SIS informant. How she discovered Hans on her doorstep and ultimately saved his life. She had given the British intelligence regarding the supply shipments, which led to their arrest.

She told him everything, every little detail gushing from her lips like a flash flood after a downpour. She couldn't have stopped herself if she tried, but she didn't want to. She had no idea how much she had kept hidden, unwilling to give anybody the whole truth. It felt good to confess everything now, even if it was to a Gestapo official whose only purpose was to use everything against her.

S.S. Weston took up the tape recorder. The brightness of the red light faded away as he turned it off, signifying the conclusion of their interview. He got to his feet and walked for the door.

"Where are you going?" She questioned, pulling herself up from the mattress.

"I'll be back," he said. His tone was cold and emotionless as the cell door closed behind him.

His face had remained the same when she told him what she knew. He had asked just a few questions, allowing her to talk freely until she felt she was done.

She expected him to gloat, or at least to have a pleased look on his face since she had given up. There had been none of it, however. He'd merely sat there, listening with a distant expression in his eyes, as if he were plotting his next move. However, none of them could make any more movements. This was the end of the line, the last game. They were both aware that it had always been this way. Perhaps he was attempting to determine what dreadful destiny might await her? Firing squad? No… too fast and neat, she reasoned. It was more probable that they would be transported off to a concentration camp. They would want her to suffer as long as possible.

She shrugged off the terrible idea. Hans had a plan. He needed to have a plan. Why else would he have instructed her to tell them what she knew? He needed to know what it meant and what would happen.

She sat back down on the bed and pushed herself back till her back was against the wall. She pulled her legs to her chest, put her arms over them, and rested her head on the tops of her knees. He had a plan. She repeated those phrases in her brain, willing herself to believe them.

She closed her eyes and remained in that posture for what seemed like hours until the cell door eventually opened. S.S. Weston waited at the doorway, his eager gaze on her.

He indicated for her to rise, and she did so, hesitating only slightly as he motioned for her to approach him. He guided her along the passage, pressing his fingers against her back. A shudder ran down her spine as they passed the questioning room. Whatever was in store for her, she was willing to accept it if it meant never having to enter that room again. She let her thoughts wander as they passed each chamber, traveling through strange passageways until they came to a massive metal door.

S.S. Weston's hand left her back and wrapped securely around her upper arm. She saw a flash of metal as he withdrew something from his pocket. Handcuffs. S.S. Weston pulled her hands together in front of her and fastened the shackles around her wrists. She swallowed. She should have been scared of what was beyond the door, but she wasn't.

S.S. Weston opened the door, which creaked. Goose bumps appeared on her skin as a rush of chilly air swept over her hair. She squinted, her eyes adjusting to the last ray of sunshine that appeared over the horizon. It was nightfall, but the winter sun shone brighter than the low, fluorescent lights she had become used to. She trembled as another cold passed through her. She didn't care, however. She delighted in the sensation. It'd been weeks since she'd seen the sun or breathed fresh air.

S.S. Weston drew her forward, her feet stumbling as she tried to keep up with him, the cold exacerbating her already hurting muscles. They had scarcely traveled a few steps when Olivia heard the crunch of gravel. As it drew into the lot, a jeep appeared, with its convertible canvas top drawn up to protect its occupants from the cold. The car came to a halt in front of them, and the driver's and passenger's side doors opened to show two guys.

She first encountered Lieutenant Hayes's black gaze. As he pulled himself up against the open passenger side door, he narrowed his eyes at her and smirked, bringing the corners of his lips up. She averted her gaze, focused on the second guy as he moved around the truck, approaching them. Hans's blue eyes momentarily met hers before drifting down her body, his jaw tightening as he examined each mark on her exposed skin.

She gazed down, focusing her gaze on the rough earth beneath her. He'd stared at her in that manner previously, when she was assaulted by the soldier in the alleyway. He pitied her, and she despised it. She hated how fragile and feeble she seemed. She despised how fragile and feeble she felt.

"S.S. Weston," she heard Hans yell out as the guys exchanged pleasantries.

"Captain Friedrich," S.S. Weston responded. Keeping one hand loosely over her arm, he offered the other to Hans. "I'm afraid we haven't met," S.S. Weston told Lieutenant Hayes, as she anticipated.

"This is Lieutenant Hayes," Hans responded for him. "He serves in the War Office as a liaison between the labor camps on the Western Front. He'll be our official escort to Vught," he said with a tinge of displeasure in his voice.

"Wouldn't want to break protocol after all," Lieutenant Hayes replied, a sneer visible in his voice.

"Alright," S.S. Weston said, nodding. "Let's not spend any more time with niceties. I'd prefer not be on the road all night.

So, this was his strategy... Break her out while she was being transferred to a concentration camp? She had no clue how he expected to do this with a Gestapo officer and Lieutenant Hayes trailing along. Had he known they'd be joining them? Or was this just an unanticipated setback in his plan? Did he have a backup plan in case this went wrong?

She was taken out of her thoughts when S.S. Weston pushed her forward, towards the jeep's backdoor. Lieutenant Hayes unlocked the door and hoisted her into the backseat, then attempted to jump in after her.

"What are you doing?" Hans inquired, standing between him and the truck.

"I just thought I'd give the two higher-ranking officers the front seats," Lieutenant Hayes said innocently. Hans paused, glancing over his shoulder, briefly focusing on Olivia before moving out of Lieutenant Hayes's way.

She slid across the bench seat until she was seated on the driver's side, wanting to put as much distance as possible between herself and Lieutenant Hayes. Lieutenant Hayes slipped into the backseat and closed the door, inching towards Olivia until their shoulders met. She clenched her jaw, her stomach turning upside down with disgust as memories of their previous encounter flooded her mind. She sat motionless as Hans and S.S. Weston took their seats in the front.

Hans shifted the jeep into gear and drove out of the lot onto the road.

"Are you cold?" Lieutenant Hayes inquired, his breath hot on her ear. She shrugged and pressed herself against the door.

"Leave her alone," Hans said, his tone more irritated than furious.

"What?" Lieutenant Hayes smirked. "She might as well be wearing nothing but her shift because this dress is so thin," he said, pinching the fabric's hem with his fingers. He released it and rested his hand against her knee. She pulled in a deep breath and looked in the rearview mirror.

Hans's eyes were fixed on the road, his expression unreadable. She looked away, out the window. According to their surroundings and the rugged, bumpy road they were now driving down, they were on a service road to Vught. The old factories and shipping yards they'd driven past had been replaced by tall, skinny pine trees on either side of the road, with the swaying branches almost completely blocking the dim glow of the sunset.

Hans had never felt more distant from her, despite the fact that she was only a few feet away. She had desperately wanted to run to him as soon as she saw him. To cling to him and not let go.

"You have a part to play," she reminded herself. You both do. Hans would somehow get her out of this. She trusted that... She had no option but to.

She was startled from her thoughts when the jeep came to a halt.

"What's going on?" Lieutenant Hayes asked. He removed his hand from her knee and braced it against the front seat, preventing himself from propelling forward. With her bound hands, she peered over the front seat.

There was a vehicle parked horizontally on the road, preventing them from passing. The automobile was turned on, and the headlights shone into the trees, but no one seemed to be inside. Hans moved the vehicle to park.

Opening the door, he got out of the front seat, followed closely by S.S. Weston. Hans looked over his shoulder, between Olivia and Lieutenant Hayes.

"Stay here."

22

CHAPTER TWENTY-TWO

Olivia stared from the rear seat as Hans and S.S. Weston approached the car. She couldn't tell the specific make or model from the brightness of the headlights, but it didn't seem to be military. If not the military, then who? Why would someone park their automobile in the midst of a remote service route and ditch it while still running? The whole scene made her skin tingle with chills. Something wasn't right. This did not seem right.

Four people came from the forest line, rifles aimed squarely at Hans and S.S. Weston. It was an ambush. Was it a raid by the Dutch resistance?

She squinted, attempting to figure out what the guys were wearing in the low light that the sun was still able to shine over the trees. They donned black overcoats to match their military fatigues, with a green beret atop each man's head. These guys were not part of the Resistance.

"We know you've got one of ours in there," One of the males spoke in a fancy British accent, nodding toward the vehicle. "Give her to us, and we'll let you be on your way."

Her heart skips a beat. They were here for her. This was part of the plan, or was it?

She was startled from her thoughts as an arm slid around her neck, tugging her from the backseat. Cold metal brushed against her skull as Lieutenant Hayes drew her into his body. The troops' eyes and rifles flashed in their way, drawing everyone's attention to Olivia and the handgun Lieutenant Hayes was holding to her head.

"If you want her, come get her," Lieutenant Hayes hissed, placing his chin on top of her head.

"Let the girl go," One of the guys shouted loudly, his rifle pointing directly at Lieutenant Hayes.

"Or what?" Lieutenant Hayes inquired, tightening his arm around her as one of the guys approached them.

"Will you shoot me? I doubt any of you can shoot me without killing her." He pointed to Hans and S.S. Weston, who exchanged a quick glance before dropping their raised hands in submission. They approached Lieutenant Hayes, surrounded him, and then turned to face the guys, whose rifles were still aimed in their direction.

"Give her to us, and we'll let you go on about your business," The same guy, who she assumed was the leader, spoke again.

"I think we all know that's a lie," Lieutenant Hayes said matter-of-factly. "The moment we turn her over to you, we'll all get a bullet in the head."

"Daan't confuse us wif your kind," Another soldier spoke out, his accent heavier and less formal than his opponent. "We daan't give a man our word and then shoot 'im in the bloody back."

The commander raised a hand, instructing the soldier to cease speaking.

"All cards are on the table," he said, returning his focus to Lieutenant Hayes. "You are outnumbered... There's a sniper in the tree line waiting for you to make the wrong move," he said, pointing to the trees. "All I have to do is give the go-ahead, then bang," he said, smiling pleasantly. Was he lying, or was there a sniper lurking somewhere in the darkness?

"It'll be hard for you to give that signal if I put a bullet in you first," Lieutenant Hayes hissed, taking the barrel of his rifle away from her body and directing it in the man's direction.

Lieutenant Hayes's body went limp to the ground, leaving a harsh thump behind her. Spinning around, her gaze was drawn to S.S. Weston, who stood over Lieutenant Hayes, the buttstock of his rifle still rising from where he had hit him in the back.

"He wasn't part of the plan," he said Hans, pushing Lieutenant Hayes's rifle out of reach.

"The plan?" Her brow wrinkled as she struggled to understand what was going on. "You two know each other?"

"Ernst's an old friend," Hans acknowledged with a nod.

"We met at university," S.S. Weston stated.

"And once the war broke out, we enlisted together," he said.

"Was this always the idea, then? You knew the entire time?" She inquired, turning to S.S. Weston. This was too weird for her mind to absorb.

"Captain Friedrich approached me after that first day, and asked for my help," he told me. So that's why he hadn't hit her after the first day, she reasoned, finally making sense of the situation.

"Once I knew I had help on the inside, I set my sights on the SIS," he said. "Getting in touch with the right people took time,

though... Time I wish I hadn't had to take," he said, running his fingers over a bruise on her face that had started to yellow.
"Why would you help him?"
"He saved my brother's life in France," S.S. Weston said, offering Hans an earnest look of appreciation that Olivia felt was genuine.
"He was one of the men on the minefield," she said, rather than asking a question. Hans nodded. The terrible irony of the situation did not escape her... The fact that he had rescued another person's sibling but had failed to save his own. And now, 'someone' had helped save her life.
"I hate to break up this little reunion, but we need to be going, we don't want any more unwelcomed guests turning up at the party." Said the leader of the group.
Hans took Olivia's hand and led her over to the group of guys, their guns now holstered rather than pointing in her way. Without suddenly, one of the soldiers seized Hans and sucker punched him hard in the jaw.
"What are you doing?!" She shouted, staring in horror as the soldier resumed his attack with a knee to Hans's stomach. "Stop!" She pulled herself between them, keeping Hans safe behind her.

"It's fine," Hans shook his head. He straightened erect, leaning on her shoulder and wiping away the blood that had flowed from the wound in his temple. "If we're going to say we were ambushed, we'll have to make it look believable."

"Don't want anyone asking too many questions," S.S. Weston muttered, his voice nasally as he squeezed the bridge of his nose to stem the nosebleed caused by one of the other men's blows to his face.

"Give us a moment," she said, turning to face the group's leader. His eyes and hair were dark brown, and his jaw stern. He reminded her of Harold. "Please," she said, as he gave her an aggravated expression that reminded her of Harold.

"Make it a quick one," He eventually said. Turning on his heel, he moved a few steps away, motioning for his soldiers to follow.

"Are you okay?" She inquired, running her fingers over the cut on Hans's forehead.

"I've had worse," he said. He grasped her hand and dropped it to his chest, keeping it there.

"Are you okay?" He questioned, looking down at her.

She nodded; her lips curled into a half-hearted grin.

"I'm very sorry," he said. His gaze strayed from hers, scouring her body for the bruises they both knew there.

"If I could have carried you out of that horrible place the very first day, I would-"

"It doesn't matter," She shook her head and pressed her face to his. "You are here now... That is all that matters." They remained there for a time, neither saying anything, until she found the nerve to pose the question she had been thinking about. "In your letter," she said, taking in a nervous breath. "You said, 'until we say goodbye'... Is this what you intended?"

Hans nodded.

"I don't want to leave you," she whispered, straining her teeth to hold back the tears.

"But you have to," he said matter-of-factly. "They've arranged passage for you to London, and these men will ensure you make it there safely."

She gazed up at him, her forehead furrowed in a state of doubt.

"They'll take care of you," he reassured.

"Will I ever see you again?" Her voice had practically dropped to a whisper.

"I'll find my way back to you... I always will," he whispered, stroking her face with his palm. "I swear it," he said, pushing his other hand to her stomach.

"Hans..." She stopped, attempting to find the words. "I'm really sorry... All the pain I've caused... All the-"

"You could cut my heart out, and it would still beat for you," he interrupted, now cradling her face with both hands. "I love you," he told her, looking into her eyes. He wrapped his arms around her and drew her into a tight embrace. She threw her arms around his waist and returned the hug. She refused to let go... She never wanted to leave his arms again. She had to, however.

"Will you write?" It was a foolish inquiry, but she wanted the comfort.

"Everyday," he replied, brushing her hair.

"Time's up," the dark-haired guy said.

She wiped the tears from her eyes as she pulled away. What little time they had left was passed, and it was time to go. Hans pushed her head up to meet his gaze, clutching her chin.

"You're in every line I've ever read," he said softly, brushing his lips against hers. "I love you."

"I love you, too," she said as his lips left hers. As she turned to go, she grabbed his hand and squeezed it one final time before it slid out of grasp.

EPILOGUE

October 14, 1944.

Hans,

"I hope you're well. I heard in the papers that the Americans had breached German lines in West Holland. And, although I hope this means we're one step closer to the conclusion of the conflict, I'm scared about you. Sophia is expanding more than ever. She enjoys looking at images of you. Every day, she requests to visit "Dada." I yearn for the day when she may meet her father and you, your daughter. Until then, we extend all of our love."

- Oliv

She put down the pen and held up the piece of paper to study it. She got to her feet, the chair legs ripping over the floor as she approached the door.

"I'm going to the mailbox," she said over her shoulder to Grace, who was preparing supper in the kitchen. She opened the door and went outside, beginning the short stroll down the cobblestone path that led to the end of the driveway.

She gazed about, allowing her thoughts to wander as she took in the light given by the sunset over the orange and red colors of the landscape.

It had been a year and a half since she had left Holland. She'd climbed into that Jeep and watched Hans's form fade from view in the rearview mirror. She had felt so many emotions that day. She was relieved to have made it out alive, but she was also terrified of what was to follow and having to face it all without Hans.

The British troops who had rescued her had been at her side the whole time, yet she had never felt more alone in her life. Hans had been correct, however. She had to go. As much as it grieved her, she no longer had a home in Holland.

Petrified and devastated, she boarded the boat that would carry her to a port just east of Colchester, where Grace was waiting. They'd settled down in a modest cottage that Grace had been renting with the money she'd earned working at the weapons plant. Despite her lack of formal training, Olivia had secured a position with a doctor, working in the clinic he owned in the center of town. She gave birth to Sophia five months later.

She and Hans had corresponded often, but despite the words and images sent by mail, his absence was evident.

She resented the fact that Sophia had gone a year without meeting her father. She had taken her first steps... and spoken her first words. All without Hans present to see it. Birthdays, Christmas... Every holiday and milestone that passed made her heart throb even more.

Sighing, she opened the mailbox and slipped the letter inside.

"Is that for me?" A voice called from behind. Turning on her heel, she saw a familiar set of blue eyes.

"Hans," she said breathlessly. He stood only a few yards away, his mouth curled into the crooked grin she knew so well. She ran to him as the gap between them narrowed, wrapped her arms securely around his neck. He dropped the bag he was carrying and reciprocated the hug, burying his face in her hair. She finally relaxed her arms enough to look up at him fully.

"Wha-what are you... How?" She stuttered, fumbling over words while attempting to make sense of it all.

Hans answered, "Den Haag has been taken by the Allies. I was relieved of my post, effective immediately," he said, reverting to his previous cheeky grin.

"They just let you leave?" She asked incredulously.

"It seems a few of your friends in the SIS remembered me," he said with a chuckle. "There was some red tape to cut through, but as soon as they released me, I got on the first boat I could charter."

"What about your family?" She asked, her thoughts racing in a million different ways.

"They left for America in May," he said. "They wrote me last month saying they'd settled somewhere called Philadelphia."

"I can't believe you're here," she said, shaking her head. He was truly here. She cupped his face in her hands and crushed her lips on his. He reciprocated her kiss, pulling her firmly against him.

"Olivia, Char is asking for y-," Grace yelled from the driveway, holding Sophia on her hip, but she paused as her gaze landed on Hans. "Who's this?" She inquired, looking between Olivia and the mystery guy whose arms were still wrapped around her waist.

"Grace," she said, moving to the side. "This is Hans Friedrich."

"The Captain Friedrich?" Grace cocked an eyebrow.

"This is my sister," Olivia said, gesturing toward Grace.

"Grace," Grace replied, reaching out her free hand to Hans.

"I've heard quite a bit about you," Hans said, grasping her hand.

"All good things, I hope," she grinned coyly.

"Of course," he said, matching her sly grin.

"Will you be staying for dinner?" She asked, passing Sophia to Olivia.
"I...," he looked to Olivia for a response. "If that's alright."
"Of course, it is," Grace interjected before she could respond. "I'll set an extra place at the table." With that, she turned on her heel and returned inside.
"There's someone I suppose you'd like to meet," she added when they were alone again. Sophia gazed up at Hans as she shifted her weight to rest on her hip. "This is Sophia."
"The pictures didn't do her justice," he said, his gaze fixed on the little blue eyes staring up at him. "She's beautiful."
"Would you like to hold her?"
"Can I?" He asked tentatively.
"Of course," she said, smiling reassuringly. "She's yours after all."
He nodded awkwardly and removed her from Olivia's arms.
"Hello, Sophia," He smiled down at her, taking in every detail of her face, not wanting to miss anything. "She looks like you," he said, gazing up at Olivia.
"She has your eyes," she told her daughter, tucking a wispy hair behind her ear.
"Dinner's ready," Grace said from the front door.
"I suppose that's our cue," he added.
"I suppose so."

Hand in hand, they went up the driveway. She opened the front door and walked inside, but stopped when Hans did not follow.

"What is it?" She returned his stare with anticipation.

"I love you," he said. He drew her close, wrapping his free arm around her and kissing her on the forehead.

"I love you, too," she said. She closed her eyes and rested her head on his chest, never wanting to leave his arms again.

The End......

Author Note

Thank you for reading one of my books. This is my 5th book. I would love to hear your honest opinion about the book in a review/suggestion for me to read. I wish to make improvements in subsequent books based and make my work more appreciable to you and others.

If you enjoyed this novel, I have recommended more of my books in the next page. You can also follow me for updates on my new releases and find more of my books.

Recommended Reads

WORLD WAR II HOLOCAUST FICTION SERIES

Forbidden Bonds of Auschwitz (Book 1)

Forbidden Bonds of Auschwitz (Book 2)

The Secret Courier (Book 1)

The Secret Courier (Book 2)

War's Embrace

A Silent Heart

I Am Daliah

About The Author

I am a storyteller with a knack for finding the extraordinary in everyday life. Hailing from a small town, I bring a down-to-earth charm to the world of fiction, where relatable characters navigate the twists and turns of life in compelling and authentic ways.

I draw inspiration from the simplicity of my small-town living and the complexity of human relationships, I try to make my stories resonate with readers who appreciate the beauty found in the ordinary. With a writing style that is approachable and engaging, I have crafted narratives that capture the essence of the human experience.

Whether exploring the dynamics of family, delving into the challenges of modern relationships, or simply observing the quirks of daily life, my stories are grounded in a realism that makes them both accessible and compelling.

Printed in the USA
CPSIA information can be obtained
at www.ICGtesting.com
LVHW090810210924
791741LV00029B/238